# TALES OF MYSTERY & IMAGINATION

From the Stories by EDGAR ALLAN POE

Retold by Tony Allan

With introduction and notes by Anthony Marks

Illustrated by Barry Jones

First published in 2002 by Usborne Publishing Ltd,
Usborne House, 83-85 Saffron Hill, London
EC1N 8RT, England.
www.usborne.com

A catalogue record for this title is available from
the British Library

Printed in Great Britain

Edited by Kamini Khanduri & Anthony Marks
Designed by Brian Voakes
Series editors: Jane Chisholm & Rosie Dickins
Cover design by Neil Francis
Cover image: Alexis Rodrigues-Duarte/Nonstock
Inc./Photolibrary.com

# CONTENTS

About Tales of Mystery and Imagination   5

The Masque of the Red Death   9

Manuscript Found in a Bottle   19

The Pit and the Pendulum   32

Metzengerstein   49

The Telltale Heart   59

The Fall of the House of Usher   68

The Gold Bug
Part one: *Treasure Hunt*   86

The Gold Bug
Part two: *The Key to the Mystery*   105

More About Edgar Allan Poe   121

# About Tales of Mystery and Imagination

These creepy, spine-tingling tales were written by the American author and critic, Edgar Allan Poe. Poe was born in Boston in 1809. His parents, both actors, died when he was very young, and he was brought up by foster-parents, John and Frances Allan, in Richmond, Virginia. In 1827, at the age of eighteen, he published his first book of poems. After a brief period in the army, he moved to Baltimore for four years, where he published one of his first stories, "Metzengerstein". Later, he held a number of jobs as newspaper editor and critic in different American cities, and his poetry and stories appeared regularly in a variety of magazines and newspapers. His writing received some critical acclaim, but it was never a huge success in his own lifetime. Poe died mysteriously in 1849, aged only forty, in circumstances which have never been fully explained.

Poe's stories appeared in around thirty different publications during his lifetime. After his death, they were collected in book form as *Tales of Mystery and Imagination*. This title reflects the variety of subjects they cover. The tales range from straightforward mystery thrillers, such as "The Gold Bug", to horror stories like "The Pit and the Pendulum", with its detailed description of physical and mental torment. "Manuscript Found in a Bottle" explores the supernatural and distortions of time and memory, while "The Telltale Heart" looks at the workings of the mind and psychological terror.

At this time, most authors were writing traditional novels with long, complicated plots and a large cast of characters. Poe was one of the first to concentrate on short stories instead. Other writers were also experimenting with short stories, particularly the 'sensational' ghost and horror tales that were becoming popular in newspapers and magazines. But Poe was critical of these, and published a number of articles mocking this style of writing for being shallow and predictable. Though his stories tackled sensational subjects too, he developed a rather different style, and his work is often now seen as the start of a new American literary tradition.

In Poe's stories, the writing is very concentrated, with often only two or three characters, sometimes just one, described very carefully. The action often takes place in a small or confined space – the dungeon in "The Pit and the Pendulum", or the abbey in "The Masque of the Red Death", for example – but is so vividly described that it creates an unforgettable atmosphere. The story usually unfolds very quickly, and is based around a single memorable event, like the fire in "Metzengerstein". Poe's powers of description mean that we very quickly grasp the people, the places and the plot.

Another important feature of the stories is that they are written so that it is easy to understand and share the emotions of the characters. Feelings are described just as vividly as people and places. Poe's tales convey very powerful sensations, such as fear, guilt, elation, sadness and confusion – things everyone has experienced at some time or other. Poe was able to make his readers feel these things along with his characters. This is why his *Tales of Mystery and Imagination* continue to fascinate readers today.

# THE MASQUE OF THE RED DEATH

For many years, the country had been in the grip of the Red Death. No plague before had ever been so deadly or so hideous. Blood was its distinguishing mark – the redness and horror of blood. Its first symptoms were sharp pains and sudden dizziness. Then blood would seep out of the victim's pores, leaving a red mark below the surface of the skin. These scarlet stains on the body, and particularly on the face, made it impossible for sufferers to remain anonymous. This meant they received little help or sympathy from others who feared becoming infected themselves. The plague struck with lightning speed – within half an hour of catching it, a person could die.

But the ruler of the land, Prince Prospero, was not concerned. As the death toll rose, he chose a thousand healthy knights and ladies from his court, and commanded them to go with him to an enormous abbey, that had been built according to his orders in a remote and secluded spot. Strong walls and gates of iron guarded it, and once the Prince and all his courtiers were inside, the huge gates were welded shut. No stranger carrying the disease could get in, but for those inside there was no way out.

Inside the abbey, the Prince's courtiers had everything that they could possibly want or need. There was plenty to eat and drink, and the Prince had been careful to provide all sorts of entertainment so no one would get bored. There were storytellers, clowns, dancers and musicians. Beauty, pleasure and, above all, safety reigned within the abbey walls. The Red Death lurked outside.

Five or six months after he had shut himself off from the world, with the plague still raging all around, Prince Prospero decided his guests needed something spectacular to entertain them. He made arrangements for a magnificent masquerade ball – a ball where everyone would dress up in amazing costumes, with their faces hidden by masks.

The ball was to be held in a suite of seven chambers in the abbey. Each chamber had a window of stained glass that looked out onto a winding corridor. There was no lamp or candle in any of the chambers, but in the corridor stood tripods holding burning torches, one in front of each window.

Every chamber was decorated in a different shade, with the glass in its window matching the decorations. So the first chamber was all in blue, and the torchlight passing through the glass cast a sky-blue glow across its floor and walls. The second chamber was purple, the third was green, the fourth, fifth and sixth were orange, white and violet.

Only in the last of the seven rooms was the window glass a different shade from the decorations. The chamber itself was shrouded in black velvet tapestries that hung all over the ceiling and down the walls, falling in heavy folds upon a black velvet carpet. But the window was scarlet – a deep blood red. The effect of the torchlight streaming through the blood-tinted panes onto the dark hangings was ghastly in the extreme, and threw such a weird light onto the faces of all who entered, that few were bold enough to set foot within that room.

Against the far wall of this last chamber there was a huge clock made of ebony wood. Every time the minute hand completed its circle of the face, the clock

struck the hour with a clear, deep sound. Its tone was so strange that the musicians stopped playing for a moment and the dancing would grind to a halt. Even the wildest of the courtiers grew pale, while those who were older and more sedate seemed lost in sudden thought.

Then the echoes of the chime would die away, and people would dismiss their fears with a laugh. The musicians would smile at each other and whisper that, next time, they would pay no attention to the striking of the clock. But after sixty more minutes had passed and the chimes came again, there was exactly the same momentary disturbance. It was as if the sound brought to mind dark thoughts of the world outside and the passage of time.

In spite of all these interruptions, it was a splendid and magnificent revel. All the trappings of the ball reflected the Prince's own tastes, which were strange and original to say the least. Prospero had a fine eye for visual effects, and his ideas were bold and fiery. Just as he had designed the furnishings of the seven chambers, so he had also had a hand in thinking up the dancers' costumes. These were grotesque creations, which had been put together with much glitter and gaudiness and wild imagination. Many of them were beautiful but also bizarre – and even a little frightening.

As the masked dancers moved from one chamber of the ball to the next, their faces changed from sky blue to deep purple, and then to green, and so on. They writhed to and fro, and the wild music seemed to reflect their weird twisting movements. And then the ebony clock would strike, and for a moment everything would fall still. The dancers would stand rooted to the spot. But as the echoes of the chime died away, light, half-subdued laughter would float above the crowd, and the music would swell up again. The dancers would come back to life, merrier than ever, lit up eerily by the strange light streaming through the stained-glass windows.

Yet none of the dancers now dared to venture into the last chamber. For, as night drew on, the light coming through the blood-tinted panes seemed all the redder, and the blackness of the draperies all the more gruesome. And the sound of the clock's chimes seemed more sinister to those who had stood on the black velvet carpet than it ever did to those in the more distant rooms.

But all the other chambers were packed full and throbbed with life. The revel whirled on and on, until at last the clock began to strike midnight. And then the music stopped and the dancers fell quiet and still. It was just as it had been every previous time the clock had struck the hour. Only now there were twelve strokes to be sounded: more time for those dark thoughts – and more time, too, for people to become aware of a masked figure that no one had noticed before.

Word of the new arrival was passed around in whispers, until at last a buzz arose from the whole gathering, expressing first surprise and disapproval, and then horror, disgust and fear. It had to be something quite extraordinary to have so great an effect on such a wildly-dressed crowd. Almost anything was acceptable at Prince Prospero's masquerades, but the newcomer had overstepped even these limits. It seemed to the guests that he had made a joke of the one thing they all knew was no laughing matter. He appeared to be mocking the Red Death itself.

His body was tall and gaunt, and he was shrouded from head to foot in grave-clothes. His mask looked like the face of a stiffened corpse. The courtiers might have put up with all this as a jest in poor taste. But the stranger had gone even farther. He had sprinkled his costume and his mask with drops of blood, as if he were suffering from the plague.

Finally the Prince himself caught sight of this strange character stalking to and fro among the dancers. He was seen to shudder, either with fear or disgust. But almost at once his face turned red with rage.

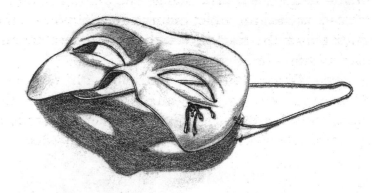

"Who dares insult us with this vile mockery?" he asked the courtiers standing near him. "Seize him and take off his mask. That way we'll know who it is we're hanging when we string him from the battlements at sunrise."

As he uttered this threat, the Prince was standing in the first chamber. He had waved a hand to silence the music, so his voice rang out loud and clear through all the seven rooms. Spurred on by the Prince's words, the courtiers around him made a rush at the stranger. But instead of trying to escape, he turned to face the Prince and approached him with a stately and deliberate step.

An inexplicable awe seemed to fall upon the bystanders, and no one put out a hand to stop the masked figure as he passed by. The stranger came within a yard of the Prince, then moved on. As he advanced, the crowd shrank back against the walls. They cleared a path for him to pass unhindered, first from the blue room into the purple, and then on in turn through the green, orange and white chambers. He had reached the violet room and was almost on the threshold of the final, black chamber before anyone tried to stop him.

Then Prince Prospero, seething with rage and ashamed of his own cowardice, rushed after the intruder with a drawn dagger in his hand. Transfixed by terror, the courtiers made no attempt to follow.

The Prince was within three or four feet of his target when the stranger suddenly turned to confront him. A cry rang out and the dagger fell onto the black carpet. A moment later, the Prince fell too. He was dead.

The courtiers now drew courage from despair. A crowd of them surged into the black chamber and threw themselves upon the stranger, who was standing erect and motionless in the shadow of the ebony clock. But they quickly fell back in horror when they found that there was nothing there for them to grab hold of – no body inside the grave-clothes and no face behind the mask.

Then they realized that the Red Death itself was in the room. It had come like a thief in the night. One by one they dropped in the blood-stained halls of their revel, dying as they fell. The ticking of the ebony clock ceased as the last of the merrymakers passed away. And the flames of the torches were extinguished. Then Darkness and Decay and the Red Death ruled unchallenged over all.

# Manuscript Found in a Bottle

There's not much to tell about my family or where I come from. Let's just say that I had an unhappy childhood, but that I left it all behind me long ago. I had a good education though, and from an early age I was interested in learning the truth about things. I love logic and order, and have always disliked superstitious tales.

I'm telling you all this in case you should think the story I am about to tell is simply the product of a wild imagination. Nothing could be farther from the truth. I'm not a dreamer, and the incredible events I describe all really happened. As I write this, I know that my words may never be read, but I will do what I can to preserve them. If all else fails, I shall put the manuscript in a bottle and throw it into the sea.

Much of my life has been spent on journeys. After many years abroad, I sailed one day from a port on the island of Java, on a boat that was headed for the Sunda Islands. Our vessel was a beautiful ship of about four hundred tons, and it carried a cargo of oil and coconuts. There was hardly a breath of wind when we got under way, and we spent many days moving very slowly along Java's eastern coast.

One evening on deck, I spotted a strange-looking cloud on the horizon to the northwest. It was the first cloud we had seen since leaving port, and there was something peculiar about it. I watched it carefully until sunset, when all at once it spread eastward and westward, cloaking the horizon in a long hazy line that could easily have been mistaken for a flat beach.

I couldn't help noticing that, soon after this, the moon came up a dusky red and that something strange seemed to be happening to the sea. The water looked unusually transparent, and in the glow of late twilight I could see right to the bottom, even though it was ninety feet below.

The air now became unbearably hot, and little spirals of steam like those given off by a hot iron were rising from the surface of the water. As night came on, the last breath of wind died away. There was total calm, without even enough of a breeze to stir a candle flame.

The stillness made me nervous. It was just the kind of calm that sometimes comes before a tropical storm. But the captain saw no sign of danger. He gave orders for the sails to be taken down and the anchor to be dropped for the night.

I went below to my cabin, troubled by a sense of impending disaster. I had told the captain about my fears, but he paid no attention, not even bothering to reply. But I couldn't sleep for worrying, so around midnight I made my way back up onto the deck.

I had just reached the top of the stairs leading up to the deck when I was startled to hear a loud humming, like the noise a mill-wheel makes when it is turning very fast. Before I could guess what the sound was, I felt the ship shaking violently. In the next instant, a wild torrent of foam swept over the entire deck from bow to stern. A huge wave had turned the boat on its side.

The masts broke immediately and the ship began to fill with water. But after a minute, still shuddering from the storm's blast, she somehow managed to struggle upright again.

I have no way of knowing what miracle saved me from death when the wave struck. At first, I was stunned by the shock of the water.

When I came to, I was jammed between a wooden post and the rudder. With great difficulty I managed to get to my feet and look groggily around me. The boat was surrounded by waves so mountainous that they were beyond the wildest reaches of my imagination.

After a while, I heard a voice calling. It was one of the other passengers – an old Swedish man. I shouted back as loudly as I could, and before long he came reeling along the deck to where I stood. We soon discovered that we were the only survivors. Everyone else had either been swept overboard or had drowned in their sleep when the cabins below had filled with water.

We were very nervous that the ship might still sink, but there was little the two of us could do on our own to make it more secure. The hurricane had broken the anchor cable, and the boat was now skimming along at frightening speed, with the wind behind it and the huge waves crashing over the deck. The worst of the storm was over but the wind was still very strong.

For five whole days and nights, squall after squall drove us across the water. Though not as terrible as the hurricane that had first overwhelmed us, these conditions were still fiercer than any I had met on other journeys. For the first four days, we were blown south. By the fifth day, it had become extremely cold. There were no clouds to be seen, yet the wind was increasing and blew with gusting fury.

But it was the sun that most attracted our attention. It had risen with a sickly yellow glow and hardly climbed above the horizon. All day it seemed to be giving out little of anything that could really be called light – just a dull glare. Shortly before it set, its inner glow suddenly disappeared, almost as though it had been extinguished, leaving only a dim, silvery rim to lower itself into the ocean. We waited in vain for the sun to rise again on the sixth day.

From that time on, we were shrouded in darkness, so that we could not have spotted anything even a stone's throw from the ship. We were wrapped in eternal night, and the water itself had lost the surface glitter we had grown used to in those tropical seas. We noticed, too, that there was no sign of surf or foam around us, despite the fact that the storm continued to rage as violently as ever. We were surrounded by a gloomy, suffocating blackness.

My companion was overcome by all kinds of superstitious terrors, while I slipped into a mood of silent wonder. We no longer made any attempt at all to control the ship. Fastening ourselves as best we could to the remaining stump of one of the masts, we gazed out unseeingly on a world of ocean.

With no way of telling day from night, we lost track of how long we had been drifting or where exactly we were. We only knew that we must have sailed farther south than anyone before us. The surprising thing was that we had not come to the barrier of ice that had been described in the tales of previous sailors.

Meanwhile we dreaded that every moment would be our last, and that every mountainous wave would overwhelm us. The swell was worse than anything I had ever imagined possible, and it seemed nothing short of a miracle that we didn't go under. My companion tried to cheer me up by reminding me how well the ship was made, but I had by now lost all hope of survival.

The farther we went, the more terrible the swelling of those black seas became. One moment we were carried high on the crest of some massive wave – the next, we were plunged down into the dark, watery depths at a speed that almost took our breath away.

We were at the bottom of one of these abysses when a loud cry from my companion suddenly pierced the darkness. "Look! Look!" he shouted. "Quick! Look up!"

As he spoke, I became aware of a dull red light streaming down the sides of the vast chasm in which we lay and lighting up the deck. Glancing up, I saw a sight that froze my blood. On the edge of a wave high above our heads there hovered a gigantic ship, bigger than any I had ever seen in my life. Her huge hull was a deep, dingy black, without any of the carvings that usually decorate a vessel's sides. A single row of brass cannons protruded from the gun-ports, and their polished barrels reflected the light of hundreds of lanterns swinging to and fro in the rigging. But the most astonishing thing of all was that, even in the force of that wild hurricane, the ship's sails were still aloft.

At first, we could only see her bows as she rose up on the crest of the wave. For a terrible moment she paused there, trembling and tottering. Then she swept down upon us. Somehow I found the strength to stagger back along the deck in order to avoid the full impact of the crash. The plunging vessel struck our boat in the bows, which were already almost under water, sending her to the seabed at last and taking my companion down with her. But the force of the collision hurled me through the air – straight into the rigging of the strange boat.

Unhurt, I scrambled down to the deck of the mystery vessel and was able to make my way without difficulty to the main hatchway, which was partly open. For some reason, I felt an instinctive fear of the sailors and wanted to keep away from them. So I climbed down to the hold and found myself a hiding place there.

I had scarcely settled in when I heard footsteps, and a man passed by, walking unsteadily. I couldn't see his face, but he seemed very old and frail. He groped around in a corner among a pile of dusty navigation charts and odd-looking instruments, muttering something in a language I didn't understand. Eventually he went back on deck and I saw no more of him.

I've been writing the words you have just been reading with pen and paper that I found on this terrible ship. I've been on board a long time now, and one thing I have learned is that there is no need to hide myself away. The plain fact is that my shipmates simply do not notice me. They pass by wrapped up in their own thoughts as though in a dream. Just now, the first mate looked straight at me without showing any sign that he had seen me.

About an hour ago, I summoned up the courage to join a group of the sailors. Even though I was standing right among them, they paid me no attention at all. They didn't even seem to notice that I was there. They all looked very old, just like the man I saw in the hold. Their shoulders were hunched, their hands and knees were trembling, and their wispy grey hair streamed out behind them in the wind. They spoke to each other in low, shaky voices, and around them the deck was scattered with ancient nautical instruments.

For the past few days, the ship has been continuing her headlong journey due south. She is rolling so badly that I cannot keep my footing, though the sailors seem to have little difficulty. All around there is the most appalling turmoil of water imaginable. It seems a miracle to me that the ship isn't swallowed up once and for all. Yet we glide away from waves a thousand times fiercer than any I have ever seen, as smoothly as a seagull in flight. And the colossal waters rear their heads above us like demons of the deep, but seem only able to threaten and not to destroy us.

It seems to me that we are doomed to hover

continually on the edge, without ever taking the final plunge into the abyss. The only explanation I can think of is that we are in the grip of some extremely strong current or undertow that carries us safely through the tumult.

I have been to the captain's cabin and seen the captain face to face – though, as I expected, he remained completely unaware of my presence. As I stood there watching him, I was overcome by a strange feeling of fascination. In many ways, he looked like a normal man. He was about the same height as me, and his body was sturdy and compact. But his face was extraordinary. His forehead was very smooth and hardly wrinkled at all, but there was something about his expression that suggested extreme old age. And at the same time, his grey eyes looked as if they could see far into the future.

His cabin was littered with ancient books and out-of-date, long-forgotten charts. He sat at a wooden table, poring restlessly over an old map, with his chin resting on his hand. All the time, he muttered to himself words that I didn't understand, just as the sailor in the hold had done. Even though I was standing right at his elbow, his voice sounded faint and distant, as though he were a mile away.

This ship is haunted by the spirit of the past. The sailors glide to and fro like ghosts of centuries gone by. Their eyes have an eager and uneasy look, and when I see them shining in the lanterns' wild glare, I feel a sense of distant time I have never felt before,

even though I have visited many of the ruins of the ancient world.

I described earlier how we were caught in the grip of a storm, but the battle of wind and water that now torments us makes even the words 'tornado' or 'hurricane' seem insufficient. All around is the blackness of eternal night and a chaos of foamless water. But on either side of us, two or three miles away, I can just glimpse huge walls of ice towering into the sky.

As I imagined, the ship is caught in a current – though the word scarcely seems strong enough to describe the huge tide that is carrying us south, thundering past the ice with the headlong speed of a raging torrent. I can hardly express the horror I feel. Yet at the same time I am strangely curious to discover the secrets of these unknown regions. I sense that we are hurrying ever closer to some new and thrilling discovery.

The sailors are pacing to and fro on the deck, and seem to be perpetually lost in thought. Meanwhile, the wind is still behind us. It is blowing very hard – on occasions hard enough to lift the ship right out of the water. But even as I write this, I can see that our situation is rapidly changing. To the right and left of us, the walls of ice are suddenly splitting open with a great roaring noise. We are whirling dizzily in huge circles around the walls of a gigantic column whose top is lost in darkness. I feel sure that there's not much time left. The circles are growing smaller – we are plunging madly into the whirlpool's deadly grasp. Now I can no longer hold my pen steady. Amid the roaring and bellowing and thundering of the ocean and the storm, the ship is quivering – oh help – and going down!

# THE PIT AND THE PENDULUM

The trial had lasted for so long, I was weak with exhaustion by the end of it. I had been on my feet throughout the repeated questioning, and when at last they untied me and I was allowed to sit down, I felt that I was going to faint. The words of the sentence – the dreaded death sentence – were the last clear sounds that reached my ears. After that, my captors' voices seemed to merge into one vague, distant hum. Then I heard no more.

After I came to, a long time passed in which I was only conscious of one thing – that I was still alive. Then, suddenly, I found myself able to think again. My first impulse was to try to discover where I was. But my terror at what I might find was so great that I almost sank back into unconsciousness. Gradually, life surged through me once more, and I managed to move my limbs. Finally, the memory of my trial came back – the judges, the black wall hangings of the courtroom, my descent into unconsciousness. Beyond that I remembered nothing.

So far, I had not opened my eyes. I was lying on my back and, reaching out a hand, I touched something damp and hard. I longed to look around, but dared not. It was not so much the thought of seeing horrors that alarmed me as the idea that there might be nothing to see at all.

At last, in desperation, I risked a look. My worst fears were confirmed. The blackness of eternal night lay all around me. The intensity of the darkness was stifling and the atmosphere was so unbearably close that I could hardly breathe.

I leaped to my feet, trembling from head to foot. I thrust out my arms wildly all around me. My hands touched nothing, yet I dreaded to take a step in case I should find my way barred by the walls of a tomb. I was sweating from every pore, and could feel cold beads of perspiration running down my forehead.

The suspense grew unbearable. I inched forward, with my arms stretched out in front of me, my eyes straining to catch the faintest glimmer of light. I continued in this manner for several paces, but I found nothing.

There was nothing but blackness and emptiness. Despite this, I breathed more freely, relieved that at least I hadn't been condemned to the most dreadful fate of all. I hadn't been buried in a tomb alive.

At last, my outstretched hands touched something solid. It was a wall, which was very smooth, slimy and cold, and seemed to be made of stone. I edged my way around it, fearing at every step that I would find something terrible. I soon realized, though, that in the darkness I could go on feeling my way along the wall forever, without knowing when I had returned to my starting point.

Instinctively, I reached for the knife that had been in my pocket when I was captured, but found that it was gone. So too were my own clothes. I was now dressed in a robe of coarse wool.

I had planned to push the blade of the knife into some minute crack in the wall, so I would be able to tell when I got back to my starting point. It soon struck me that I could do the same with a piece of cloth, so I tore off part of the hem of my robe and laid it on the floor, so that it was sticking out at right angles to the wall.

I had thought that exploring my prison would be an easy task, but I had not counted on the size of the area, nor on my own exhaustion. The ground was moist and slippery. I staggered on for some time, then stumbled and fell. I was too weak to get up again, and soon fell asleep where I lay.

When I woke up, I found a loaf of bread and a jug of water beside me. I was still too tired to worry about where they might have come from, so I ate and drank greedily. After a short while, I continued my tour of the prison, and with much effort finally arrived back at the piece of cloth. I had counted 52 paces to the place where I fell, and 48 more since starting off again, making 100 in all. Reckoning two paces to the yard, I estimated the dungeon to be fifty yards around. I could not guess its shape, though, for I had come across many angles.

Even though I knew there was no hope of escape, I was driven by curiosity to continue exploring. Leaving the wall, I decided to make my way across the middle of the room. At first, I moved very cautiously, because the floor was dangerously slimy. Then I summoned up my courage and stepped out boldly, trying to cross the chamber in as straight a line as I could. I had taken about ten or twelve steps when the torn hem of my robe got caught between my legs, tripping me and sending me sprawling.

For a few seconds, I was too stunned by the fall to notice a startling fact – although my chin was resting on the floor of the prison, the rest of my face was not. At the same time, a peculiar musty smell reached my nostrils and the air seemed suddenly damp and clammy. I put out an arm and shuddered to find that I was lying at the very edge of a pit whose size I had no way of guessing.

Groping around the rim of the pit, I managed to dislodge a small stone which I dropped into the abyss. For many seconds I could hear it plunging downward, dashing against the sides of the pit as it went. At last, there was a splash as it hit water. At the same moment, I heard what sounded like the rapid opening and closing of a door above my head. A faint gleam of light flashed through the gloom and then, just as quickly, vanished. I realized that my captors were listening to my every move. They had intended me to fall into the pit and were checking to see if I had. I congratulated myself on the lucky accident by which I had escaped. Another step, and that would have been the end of me.

Shaking from head to toe, I felt my way back to the wall, deciding to die there rather than risk the terror of the pits – for I now imagined there might be others scattered around the dungeon floor. For many long hours, I was too restless to sleep, but at last I managed to doze off.

When I woke up again, I found a loaf and a jug of water by my side, as before. I felt terribly thirsty, so I downed the water in one gulp. It must have been drugged, for I had scarcely finished it before I became uncontrollably drowsy. I soon fell into a deep sleep. How long it lasted I have no way of knowing, but when I opened my eyes once more, I found that I could see the objects around me. A strange, yellowish glow now lit up my prison.

I saw immediately that I had been wrong about the size of the cell. The walls were no more than 25 yards around. For some minutes, this fact worried me very much and I spent a long time trying to guess where I had gone wrong in my calculations. The truth finally dawned on me. I must have almost completed the circuit of the walls before I fell. When I woke up again, I had obviously retraced my steps in the other direction and had been too confused to realize that I had started out with the wall on my left, and ended up with it on my right.

I had also been mistaken about the shape of the prison. The many angles that I had felt were mostly no more than small cracks, and the room was basically square. What I had taken for stone walls seemed now to be huge panels of iron, and the joints of these formed the cracks. The panels were covered from top to bottom with paintings. Demons, skeletons and other hideous images glared down at me from all sides. I noticed that the outlines of the figures were quite clear, but that the paint between the lines was blurred and faded, probably from the effects of the damp atmosphere.

A quick look down at the floor showed that it was made of stone. And in the middle yawned the circular pit from whose jaws I had so narrowly escaped. Despite my earlier fears, I now saw that it was the only one in the dungeon.

I saw all this only with much effort, for my own situation had changed while I slept. I was now lying on my back, stretched at full length on a low framework of wood. I was securely tied down by a long strap that passed many times around my body and limbs, leaving only my head free – and enough of my left arm to allow me, with great difficulty, to feed myself from an earthenware dish on the floor beside me. To my horror, though, as I was terribly thirsty, I realized that the jug had been removed. I noted too that my captors meant to make me even thirstier, for the meat in the dish was very salty.

Looking up, I examined the ceiling of the prison. It was 30 or 40 feet above my head, and, like the walls, was made of metal. An extraordinary figure painted on one of its panels soon caught my eye. It was a picture of an old man with a white beard. I recognized him immediately as Old Father Time, but instead of the scythe he usually carries, he was holding what looked at first glance like a painted pendulum – a heavy brass rod with a weight at the end. Something about the appearance of this pendulum led me to examine it more carefully. As I gazed directly up at it (for it was positioned immediately above me), I thought I saw it move. The next instant I was sure. The pendulum was swinging slowly from side to side. I watched it for some minutes, partly in fear, but more in wonder. Then, tired of observing its repetitive movement, I turned my eyes away.

At this point, a slight noise attracted my attention, and I looked down to see several enormous rats crossing the floor. They were coming from the pit, which I could just make out to my right. As I watched,

they started pouring out in hordes, lured by the smell of the meat. It took a great deal of effort and energy to scare them away.

It might have been half an hour or even an hour before I looked up again. What I saw bewildered and amazed me. The sweep of the pendulum had grown wider by nearly a yard, and it was swinging faster. But what really worried me was that it appeared to be descending. I now noted with horror that the weight on the end of the pendulum was a crescent of glittering steel, about a foot long, with the ends pointing up to the ceiling and a razor-sharp blade underneath. The whole thing hissed as it cut through the air.

It didn't take me long to realize that my captors were at work again. They had originally intended me to fall to the bottom of the pit, but by sheer accident I had avoided this. I knew that all the deaths they thought up relied upon an element of surprise, so it would not have satisfied them simply to hurl me into the pit. Instead, they had designed a different method of destruction.

How can I describe the long hours of horror I spent counting every swing of the swishing pendulum? Little by little it came down, descending so slowly that it seemed to take ages for me to be sure that it actually had come lower.

Days passed – it could have been many days. At last, the blade was so close that, as it swept over me, it fanned me with its metallic breath. The smell of the steel forced itself into my nostrils. I prayed for the pendulum to come down faster and end my agony. I grew frantic, and struggled to force my body up against the sweep of the swinging steel. And then I fell suddenly calm, and lay smiling up at it, like a child fascinated by some glittering toy.

For a time I passed out, but it cannot have been for long, because when I came to, the pendulum seemed no closer. Or maybe it had been a considerable time – my captors were obviously watching me closely, and they were quite capable of halting the pendulum for just as long as I was unconscious. I now felt sick and weak, as if I had not eaten for days. For all my agony, I still wanted food. Painfully, I stretched out my left arm as far as my bonds allowed, and picked up the scraps that the rats had left me. As I put the food to my lips, I felt a small surge of joy, until the hopelessness of my situation came back to me.

The pendulum was swinging at right angles to my body. I saw that the blade had been positioned to cut across my heart. It would scrape against the coarse material of my robe not just once but many times, returning to repeat the operation again and again. It would probably take several minutes for the steel to cut through the cloth completely.

I paused at this thought. I concentrated all my attention on it, as if by so doing I could somehow stop the blade at just that point in its descent. I forced myself to imagine the sound the steel would make as

it sliced its way through the material. And I made myself think about the peculiar way in which the noise of the rubbing of cloth can grate on the nerves. I thought about all these things until my teeth were on edge.

Down – steadily down crept the blade. I took a strange, almost frenzied pleasure in comparing the incredible speed with which it swung from side to side with its dawdling downward progress. To the right, to the left, far and wide, it flew with a menacing hiss. But it moved down to my heart with the slowness of a snail.

Down – relentlessly down. Now the blade was within a hand's width of my chest. I struggled furiously to free my left arm. If I could only have undone the strap, I would have seized the pendulum and tried to stop it somehow. Yet, in my heart of hearts, I knew that it was pointless even to think of escaping.

Down – unceasingly down. I gasped and struggled each time the blade passed over me. I shrank away from every sweeping movement. With relief, my eyes followed the pendulum whenever it swung away from me, but closed instinctively as it approached again. I trembled when I thought how small an adjustment of the machinery would be necessary to drive the glistening blade straight into my heart.

I saw that it would only take ten or twelve more sweeps for the steel to touch my robe – and as I realized this, a sort of desperate calm suddenly came over me. For the first time in many hours or even days, I found myself able to think clearly.

It struck me that I was tied down by just a single strap. The first stroke of the blade over any part of the strap would sever it. Then I would only have to unwind it from my body to free myself, though that would be no easy task with the blade swinging so close. And surely my captors must have thought of this? Dreading to see my last hope extinguished, I raised my head far enough to look down over my chest. It was as I had feared. The strap had been wrapped around every part of my body – except the parts that lay in the pendulum's path.

I had hardly lowered my head when another idea started to take shape in my mind. With the nervous energy of despair, I immediately set about trying to put it into action. For many hours, the rats had been swarming around the low wooden frame on which I lay. They were wild, bold and ravenously hungry, and their red eyes glared menacingly as if they were only waiting for me to stop moving before they made me their prey.

In spite of my attempts to stop them, the rats had eaten all but a few scraps of the food in the dish. Although I kept waving my hand over it to scare them away, they had grown used to the movement. In fact, in their hunger, they sometimes even sank their sharp teeth into my fingers. Now I dabbed those fingers in the dish and rubbed what was left of the spicy meat onto the strap tied around me, wherever I could reach it. Then I lay still, hardly daring to breathe.

At first, the hungry animals were startled by the unusual stillness. They shrank back, and some returned to the pit. But this was only for a moment. Seeing that I remained motionless, one or two of the boldest jumped onto the frame and started sniffing at the strap. This seemed to be the signal for a general rush. Dozens of rats hurried over from the pit and climbed onto the woodwork. They ran all over it and scrambled onto my body. The swing of the pendulum seemed not to bother them at all. Avoiding its strokes, they started gnawing at the meat-smeared strap.

Rats swarmed over me in heaps, writhing around my throat, and I could feel their cold lips rubbing against my own. I was half stifled by their weight pressing down upon me. An unspeakable feeling of disgust came over me, sending shivers down my spine. But I could feel my bonds loosening, and I knew that in another minute the struggle would be over. With superhuman effort, I lay still.

The idea worked, and before long the strap hung from my body in tatters. But the pendulum had already brushed my chest. It had sliced through the material of my robe and reached the lining beneath. It swung twice more, and a jolt of pain shot through me. Now the moment of escape had arrived. At a wave of my hand, the rats scurried away. Moving slowly, steadily, cautiously, I slid sideways out of my bonds and eased myself away from the pendulum's reach. I was free!

But scarcely had I stepped from my bed of horror than the pendulum fell still and I saw it pulled up through the ceiling by some invisible force. I realized again that my every movement was being watched. I had escaped one form of agonizing death only to be prepared for another. With that thought in mind, I cast my eyes nervously over the iron walls that imprisoned me. Something about them seemed different. For many minutes I tried in vain to discover what it was.

I became aware for the first time where the glow that lit up the cell was coming from. It shone through a crack about half an inch wide extending all around the prison at the base of the walls, which were not attached to the floor. Crouching down, I peered through the opening but could see nothing.

As I got to my feet again, I suddenly realized what was different about the room. The previously blurred outlines of the pictures on the walls were now startlingly bright, giving the fiendish images a peculiar brilliance that would have disturbed even someone with nerves a good deal steadier than my own. All kinds of new images had appeared too, and wild demon eyes glared down on me from a thousand places where there had been none before. Then the smell of heated iron reached my nostrils. A suffocating stench began to fill the prison. All the time, the staring eyes glowed more fiercely and the burning paint shone a deeper crimson.

I panted, gasping for breath. I cowered in fear from the hot metal and inched my way closer to the middle of the cell. As I thought of the fiery destruction threatening me, the idea of the cool pit seemed almost soothing. I crawled to its rim and gazed down into its depths. The glare from the red hot roof lit up all its hideous nooks and crannies. Oh, any horror was better than that! With a shriek, I flung myself away from the edge and buried my face in my hands, weeping bitterly.

The heat was increasing rapidly. I looked up again and saw that the shape of the cell was changing. It had been square, but now the walls no longer met at right angles. They had shifted so that the room was diamond-shaped. At the same time, I could hear a low rumbling sound. There was no doubt about it – the walls were moving.

I had told myself that I preferred any death to falling into the pit. What a fool I had been! Now that was exactly where the burning walls were forcing me. What could I do to resist the glowing metal? Already the diamond was growing flatter and flatter with frightening speed. It was at its widest just around the yawning pit. I shrank back, but the closing walls were pressing me helplessly on. Soon, there was barely an inch of foothold left on the floor of the prison for my scorched feet. I gave up struggling and let out my agony in one long, loud, final scream of despair. I felt myself tottering on the edge – I closed my eyes...

Then suddenly – could this be true? – I heard the hum of voices. With a harsh, grating noise, the fiery walls rolled back. An outstretched arm caught my own just as I fell, fainting, into the pit. My captors were in the hands of their enemies.

I was free! I had been rescued!

# METZENGERSTEIN

In Hungary, long ago, some people believed in reincarnation – the idea that a dead person's soul could be born again in another body, and sometimes even in the shape of an animal.

At that time, there were two noble and wealthy families living near each other. So near, in fact, that the windows of the palace of the Metzengersteins even overlooked the castle of the Berlifitzings. But there was no love lost between the two. The rivalry between them stretched back over many centuries.

William, Count Berlifitzing, was a weak and doddering old man, whose hatred for the Metzengerstein family was only matched by his love of horses. Despite his age, he still insisted on going riding every day.

Frederick Metzengerstein, however, was just 17 years old. He had recently inherited the title of Baron at an unusually early age, as both his parents had died young. And he had inherited much more than a mere title. Metzengerstein Palace was just one of a dozen magnificent mansions and estates now in his possession. No other nobleman in the country owned anything like the same amount of land and property.

When the local people learned that such great wealth and power had fallen into the hands of someone with so little experience of life, they feared the worst, for Baron Frederick was already known to be rather a bad-tempered and hot-headed young man. Unfortunately, their expectations were all too quickly confirmed.

The Baron celebrated his new status with a round of wild parties that lasted several days. Large numbers of reckless young people arrived at the palace every night. And each morning they would leave, bleary-eyed and exhausted by the night's activities. During these few days, all kinds of cruel deeds were carried out against the people living nearby. The victims couldn't be sure who was to blame, but these things had never happened when the Baron's father had been alive. Then, on the fourth night, the stables at Castle Berlifitzing were set alight, apparently deliberately. The finger of suspicion quickly pointed at Frederick Metzengerstein.

News of the disaster passed rapidly around the district, and people rushed to the stables to try to stop the flames from spreading. The only person who seemed completely unconcerned by the fire was Metzengerstein himself. He sat alone in his palace, in a vast and desolate upstairs room, gazing thoughtfully at the faded tapestries that hung upon the walls.

These hangings showed portraits of his ancestors and scenes from the family's history. One detail in particular seemed to hold the Baron's attention. It was the figure of an enormous horse that had belonged long ago to one of the Berlifitzings. The beast was standing stock still in the foreground of the picture while, behind, its rider was being stabbed to death by a Metzengerstein wielding a bloody dagger.

There was something almost fiendish about the way the young Baron seemed to gloat over the scene at the very time when disaster was striking the Berlifitzing stables. Yet the longer he looked at it, the more distracted he became. It was as if he had fallen into a trance, and could not move his eyes from the horse even if he wanted to.

Then suddenly the flames of the burning buildings flared up outside, causing the Baron to turn briefly to look at the red glare flooding through the windows. A moment later, he turned his eyes back to the tapestry – and was startled to find that the horse's head appeared to have moved! Before, it had been bent down, looking sorrowfully at its dying master. Now it was raised and seemed almost to be staring out of the picture, straight at the Baron. Its eyes glowed fiery red, and its lips were drawn back in a snort of fury.

Terrified by what he saw, the young nobleman rushed to the door. As he threw it open, a flash of red light streaming in from the windows cast his shadow against the wall. He saw with horror that his silhouette exactly matched the figure of the dagger-wielding Metzengerstein in the tapestry.

Hurrying out of the palace in search of fresh air, the Baron almost bumped into three stablehands. They were struggling to control a gigantic horse, whose plunging hooves were putting their very lives at risk.

"Whose horse is that?" the Baron demanded. As he spoke, he found himself shuddering incontrollably, for

he realized at once that the animal was absolutely identical to the one he had just been looking at in the tapestry.

"He is yours, sire," one of the servants told him. "At least, no one else claims him. We caught him galloping away from the fire at the Berlifitzing stables. At first we thought he must be one of the old Count's horses. But when we took him back there, the grooms said that they'd never seen him before."

"But there was soot on his flank," one of his companions interrupted. "And if you look at his forehead, you will see there are some letters branded on it. W.V.B. – William von Berlifitzing!"

"Very strange! He certainly seems to be a remarkable beast," the young Baron mused, adding, "though he's obviously a difficult one," as the animal lashed out wildly with its hooves once more. "Still, I shall have him. A rider like Frederick of Metzengerstein should be able to tame even this devil from the Berlifitzing stables."

"But he's not from there, my lord," insisted the first servant. "The grooms swear it. We'd never have dared bring him to you if he had been."

"Hmmm. Very wise," retorted the Baron. He seemed about to say more, but at that moment he was interrupted by a page who ran out from the palace. The boy had a message for his master – something about a piece that had disappeared from one of the upstairs tapestries. He seemed upset, but he spoke so fast and mumbled so much that the stablehands were quite unable to make out exactly what it was he was saying.

All kinds of emotions raced across the Baron's face as he listened to the boy. He soon pulled himself together, though, and gave strict instructions that the room in question should be locked up at once and the key brought to him.

The stablehands were still struggling to drag the rearing horse down the long avenue that led to the Metzengerstein stables. The Baron turned to follow them, but as he did so, another messenger came running up to him.

"My Lord," he cried.

He stood in front of the Baron, gasping for breath. Finally he managed to stammer out the words, "Sir, it's Count Berlifitzing."

"Berlifitzing?" the Baron echoed. "What about him, boy?"

"He's dead."

"Dead!" A smile of satisfaction shot briefly across Metzengerstein's face. "How did he die?"

"He was trying to save the horses in his stables."

"Indeed," said the Baron calmly. "How shocking." Then he turned and strode off into the palace.

From that time on, a change came over the Baron. He remained just as ill-tempered as ever. Only now he avoided all company. He even refused to leave his own house – except to be with the strange, fiery horse. He spent his days riding it, and was rarely seen out of the saddle.

For many months, invitations continued to arrive from his friends, asking him to attend parties or to join them on boar-hunts. Briefly and rudely, he turned them all down. In time, the invitations stopped coming. Some people put the Baron's lack of courtesy down to pride, others to ill health and a gloomy temperament. A few, who had obviously forgotten how he had behaved immediately after his parents' deaths, were even charitable enough to blame it on his sorrow at losing them.

One point that everyone agreed on, though, was that his obsession with that dark and devilish horse was becoming unhealthy. No matter what the time of day or the weather, regardless even of his own state of health, young Metzengerstein would be found in the saddle of the huge beast.

Unlike the other animals in the Metzengerstein stables, the creature had no name. The Baron insisted on stabling it separately from the other horses, and he alone was allowed to feed and groom it. No one else was even permitted to enter its stall.

Gradually, people began to feel that there was something odd about the horse itself. It was seen to leap distances that no ordinary horse could manage. And sometimes there was a look in its eye from which even Metzengerstein himself shrank – a sort of quick intelligence that seemed almost human.

But no one doubted the Baron's affection for the beast – except one unimportant page to whom nobody paid any attention. This boy noticed that his master always shuddered slightly when he climbed into the saddle. And each time he came back from one of his lengthy rides, every muscle of his face would be contorted in a look of twisted triumph.

One stormy night, Baron Metzengerstein hurtled down the palace stairs and rushed like a madman out to the stables. He leaped onto the horse's back and set off in haste for the forest. None of the palace staff paid much attention at the time, for by now they were well used to their master behaving in odd ways.

A few hours later, though, they were eager enough for him to return when fire was found to be spreading through the palace. The blaze was already out of control by the time it was discovered, and it quickly became obvious that there was no hope of saving the building. Convinced that there was nothing they could do to help, a crowd of onlookers stood nearby, gazing in silent wonder.

There was a sudden stir among them when they saw Baron Metzengerstein on the giant horse, charging up the long avenue that led from the forest to the palace. He had lost his riding hat, and it was obvious from the way he sat twisted in the saddle, and from the look of agony that screwed up his features, that he was fighting unsuccessfully to control the enormous beast.

A solitary scream burst from his lips. Then the clatter of gigantic hooves echoed above the roaring of the flames and the wind's shrieking. An instant later, the horse cleared the gateway and the moat with one incredible leap. It was last seen bounding up the staircase of the palace. Then, along with its rider, it disappeared into a whirlwind of fire.

At once, the fury of the wind died away, and a deadly calm settled over the scene. Pale flames hung about the ruins of the palace, covering them like a shroud. In the fire's supernatural glare, the watching crowd saw a cloud of smoke settling heavily over what was left of the building. And as they looked on in amazement, the swirling smoke slowly shaped itself into the form of a colossal horse.

# THE TELLTALE HEART

It's true that I've always been of a nervous disposition, but I can't understand why you say that I'm crazy. If anything, nervousness has made my senses sharper, which can only be a good thing. My sense of hearing is particularly excellent. I hear all the sounds on earth, as well as most of those in heaven and hell. So how can I possibly be crazy? Listen to my story and you'll see how calm and sensible I am.

I can't say how the idea first entered my head, but once it was there it haunted me night and day. It was strange, because I wasn't angry and I had no hidden motive. Quite the opposite, in fact – I loved the old man. He had never done me any harm. And I certainly wasn't interested in his money. I think it must have been the eye! Yes, that was what it was. One of his eyes was like a vulture's, pale blue with a milky film over it. Whenever it looked at me, my blood ran cold. And so, little by little, very, very gradually, I made up my mind to take his life. That way, I would rid myself of the eye forever.

Now we come to the point. You may well think I'm mad. But madmen are fools. And you should have seen me – how cleverly I set to work, how cautiously

I laid my plans, what great care I took to hide my real intentions! In fact, I was never kinder to the old man than I was during the week before I killed him.

But every night at about midnight, I lifted the latch of his door and opened it, ever so gently. When the gap was just wide enough, I slid in a darkened lantern, one with its shutter closed so that no light shone out.

Then I put my head around the door. You would have laughed to see how cunningly I did this! I moved slowly – very, very slowly, so as not to disturb the old man as he slept. A whole hour passed before I was even far enough in to make out the shape of his body lying on the bed. You see what I mean? Would a madman have been as careful as that? And then, when my head was right inside the room, I opened the lantern's shutter, ever so gently because the hinges creaked. I opened it just enough to allow a single thin ray of light to fall upon that vulture eye.

For seven long nights I repeated this, always at around midnight. But each time, I found the eye closed, so it was impossible for me to carry out my plan. For it wasn't the old man who troubled me, you understand, just that evil eye of his.

And every morning, when day broke, I went boldly into his room and greeted him heartily, asking if he had slept well. So you see he could hardly have suspected that every night at midnight I was watching him like a hawk.

On the eighth night, I opened the door even more cautiously than usual. A watch's minute hand moves more quickly than my hand moved then. I had never realized until that moment how truly skilled I was in the art of deception. I could scarcely contain my feeling of triumph. To think that there I was, pushing open the door little by little, and that he could not even dream of what I had in mind – I positively chuckled at the thought.

Perhaps he heard me, for he moved suddenly on the bed. You may think that I drew back in alarm – but no. With the shutters fastened for fear of robbers, the room was pitch black. So I knew he could not see the door opening, and I kept on pushing, steadily, steadily. I had my head inside the room and was about to start opening the lantern, when my thumb slipped on the tin fastening. There was a sharp rattling noise and the old man sprang up in bed, crying out, "Who's there?"

I kept quite still and said nothing. For a whole hour I never moved a muscle. In all that time I did not hear him lie down. I knew he was still sitting up in bed, listening – just as I have done, night after night, hearing the tapping sound of the death-watch beetles in the wall.

Then I heard a small groan. It wasn't a groan of pain or sadness. It was the sort of low, stifled sound that comes from the depths of a mind that is overcome by fear – a groan of terror. I knew the sound well. Many a night at midnight, when the rest of the world was sleeping, I have felt that same sound echoing inside me, threatening to escape and deepening all my own fears.

So I was aware of the old man's feelings and, in a way, I felt sorry for him. But deep down I was laughing. I knew that he had been lying awake ever since the first slight noise that had made him turn in his bed. All this time, his terror had been growing. He had been trying to persuade himself it was nothing, telling himself that a mouse must have run across the floor, or that it was only the wind in the chimney. But it was no use.

When I had waited a long time, very patiently, without hearing him lie down, I decided to open the lantern just a crack. So I started moving the shutter – you can't imagine how stealthily – until at last a single faint ray, like the thread of a spider's web, shot out and fell on that vulture eye. This time the eye was open – wide, wide open! The sight of it made me insane with fury. I could see it quite clearly – all dull blue, with that hideous film over it that chilled me to the bone. But no other part of the old man's face was showing, for I had shone the ray, as if by instinct, right at that very spot.

Haven't I already told you that what you mistake for madness is really just extra-sharp senses? Maybe that was why I now heard a low, dull, quick sound – the sound a watch might make if it was wrapped up in a handkerchief. I knew that sound well too. It was the beating of the old man's heart. And it increased my fury, just as the beating of a drum spurs a soldier on. Even then, I kept absolutely still. I scarcely dared to breathe. I held the lantern motionless. I tested myself to see how steadily I could keep the ray directed on the eye. Meanwhile, the heart's vile beating grew quicker and quicker, louder and louder every moment.

I've told you before how nervous I am. And now, in the dead of night, amid the dreadful silence of the old house, that strange noise brought terror to my soul. For some minutes longer I stood still. But the beating grew louder and louder until I thought the heart would burst. Then I was seized by a new anxiety – what if the noise should wake people living nearby?

The old man's hour had come. With a sudden yell, I jerked open the lantern and leaped into the room. He shrieked once and once only. In an instant, I had dragged him to the floor and pulled the heavy mattress over him. For several minutes, the heart continued beating with a muffled sound. Then at last it stopped. I lifted up the mattress and examined the old man. There was no pulse. He was stone dead. That eye would trouble me no more.

If you still think I'm crazy, you'll soon change your mind when you hear about the care I took over hiding the body. Dawn was approaching, so I worked quickly. First of all, I cut the corpse into pieces. Then I lifted up three of the floorboards and placed the remains in the space beneath. Finally, I replaced the boards, so cleverly that no human eye – not even his! – could have noticed that anything was wrong. There were no stains to wash away, and not even a trace of blood. I had done my work well.

By the time I had finished, it was four o'clock in the morning and still pitch dark. As the clock struck the hour, there was a knocking at the street door. I went down to open it and found three men standing there. They informed me that the woman who lived next door had heard a scream during the night, and had called the police. These officers had been sent to search the house.

I smiled, for what did I have to fear? I welcomed the officers into my home and told them that it was I who had screamed, during a dream. The old man, I said, was away in the country.

I took my visitors all around the house and told them to search the place as thoroughly as they liked. Finally, I led them to his room. I showed them his possessions, all laid out in their correct places. I felt so confident that I even brought four chairs into the room and invited the men to sit down and rest. I put my own chair over the very spot where the body lay buried! The officers seemed satisfied. It must have been my manner that convinced them. I was completely at ease.

The officers sat and chatted about this and that, and I answered their questions cheerfully enough. Before long, however, I found myself wishing they would leave. My head ached, and I thought I could hear a distant ringing in my ears. But still they sat there and continued talking. The ringing seemed to be getting nearer. I chattered on, hoping the sound would go away, but it continued and grew clearer. And that was when I realized it wasn't in my ears at all. No doubt I now grew very pale, yet I kept babbling on and on. The sound grew louder. What could I do? It was a low, dull, quick sound – the sound a watch might make if it was wrapped up in a handkerchief.

In a panic, I started gasping for breath. Yet the officers seemed to hear nothing. I rose to my feet and gabbled all kinds of nonsense, waving my hands around. The sound grew louder still. Why would they not leave? I paced the floor with heavy strides, as if I were infuriated by what the men were saying. The sound kept on increasing. What could I do? I scraped my chair noisily across the floorboards, but the sound rose over everything and kept growing louder. And still the officers chatted pleasantly and smiled. Was it really possible that they did not hear it? No! They must hear. They must suspect something. They must know. Then I realized. They were making fun of my horror!

I was at a loss to know what to do. But anything seemed better than the agony I was going through, than being laughed at like that. I could bear their hypocritical smiles no longer. I felt as if I were choking. I swore, I raved like a madman, I foamed at the mouth. And still the noise grew louder, louder, louder, louder! At last I could take no more.

"Stop!" I cried. "Stop this charade. I admit everything. Everything! Tear up the floorboards – here and here. That noise – it's the beating of the old man's hideous heart."

# THE FALL OF THE HOUSE OF USHER

It was a dull, still autumn day, and the clouds hung low in the sky. Since daybreak I had been riding alone on horseback through the dreary countryside. At last, as evening drew on, I caught my first glimpse of the House of Usher. I don't know why, but as soon as I set eyes on the building, a sense of unbearable gloom came over me. The bleak walls, the empty windows staring out like eyes, the soggy clumps of marsh grass and the few, decaying trees – together all these things made up a scene that touched my heart with ice.

And yet I was planning to spend some weeks as a guest in this house. Its owner, Roderick Usher, had been one of my childhood friends. Many years had passed since we had last met, but I had recently received a letter from him. He wrote to tell me that he had been seriously ill, suffering from a disorder of the nerves.

Although we had been close as boys, I really knew very little about Usher, because he had always been shy and reserved. But he called me his best – in fact his only – friend, and he begged me to come and stay in the hope that my company would cheer him up and help him get better. The urgency of his request left no room for hesitation, so I immediately accepted this strange and unexpected invitation.

I stopped my horse on the bank of a small, steep-sided lake beside the house. Looking down, I saw the building reflected in the still, dark waters and, for some reason, this mirror image only made me shudder the more. As I looked up again, a strange idea came into my head. I began to feel that the house and its grounds had an atmosphere of their own – a sort of diseased and mysterious atmosphere – which was quite different from that of the air all around. I sensed that

it had somehow seeped out from the decaying trees and the grey walls and the silent lake.

Shaking this ridiculous thought from my mind, I began to take a closer look at the house itself. The main thing that struck me was how very old it was. A fungus-like growth had spread across the outside and hung in fine, tangled webs from the eaves. At first glance, the walls themselves looked solid enough, though the individual stones seemed to be crumbling with the passage of time. It was only after I had stared at the building for several moments that I thought I could make out an almost invisible crack, zigzagging down from the roof and losing itself in the dull waters of the lake below.

Having noted all this, I rode quickly across the bridge that spanned the lake and arrived at the main entrance of the house. A sullen-looking servant took my horse, and directed me through an arched doorway into the hall. There I was met by another servant, who led me in silence through many dark and winding passages to the room where my host was waiting to greet me.

We made our way under carved ceilings, past gloomy wall-hangings and displays of ancient weapons that rattled as we strode by. Although I had grown up in a rambling old house myself, I now found that these familiar images only increased my sense of dread and foreboding.

On one of the staircases, I met the family doctor, who, after a few brief words, hurried away. He had a sly, troubled look about him that I didn't like. Instinctively, I felt that he wasn't to be trusted. Soon after this, we reached our destination. The servant threw open a door and showed me in.

The room I found myself in was very large, with a high ceiling. The windows were tall, narrow and pointed, and set so high above the floor that there was no obvious way of reaching them. Feeble rays of crimson light made their way through the latticed panes, illuminating the larger objects nearby but leaving the far corners of the room in shadow. Dark tapestries hung on the walls, and the furniture was old and tattered. Although many books and musical instruments lay scattered about, they did not bring any life to the scene. I felt that I was breathing an atmosphere of sorrow.

As I entered, Usher got up from the sofa on which he had been lying and came to welcome me. We sat down, and I took the chance to take a good look at him. What I saw filled me with surprise. Although many years had passed since our last meeting, I had not expected to see such a change in my friend. It was hard to accept that the pale creature in front of me was the same person I had known as a boy.

His features had always been striking. He had large, luminous eyes; thin, pale, beautifully curved lips; a hooked nose with broad nostrils; a pointed chin; an unusually high forehead; hair soft as a spider's web; and a deathly white complexion. Together, all these things made up a face that was not easily forgotten.

Only now, these strange characteristics had become so exaggerated that I hardly recognized my old friend. In particular, the ghostly paleness of his skin and his wildly glittering eyes shocked me and even scared me. And his silky hair had been allowed to grow untrimmed until it floated loosely around his head in a way that looked hardly human.

And it wasn't just his appearance that was strange. Something about his manner was also far from normal. One moment he would be full of life, but the next he would become silent and gloomy. His manner of speaking was strange and disturbing too. At the start of a sentence he would sound so unsure of himself that he could hardly speak without his voice trembling,

but by the end of it he would seem oddly self-assured and even over-confident.

Despite all this, he greeted me very warmly.

"I can't tell you how glad I am to see you again," he said. "I'm sure that if anyone can help me get better, it's you."

"What exactly is the matter?" I asked, hoping to learn more details of his illness. As it happened, he was more than willing to talk about it and we were soon discussing it at length.

"The disease is hereditary in my family," he told me gloomily. "In fact, we've almost given up hope of finding a remedy." Then, seeing my anxious face, he quickly added, "But it's only a problem with my nerves. I'm sure the worst of it will soon pass."

"What are the symptoms?" I asked, feeling rather confused.

"I'm afraid there are lots of them," he replied, "but they mostly come down to one main problem. My senses are just too sharp. Because of this, I can only eat bland and tasteless foods, and my skin is allergic to dozens of different materials. The scent of flowers is enough to suffocate me, and any sort of bright light is more than my eyes can bear. As for my hearing – well, there are only a very few sounds I can listen to without a feeling of horror. Guitar music is one of them," he added, noticing my eyes straying to look at the several stringed instruments that lay scattered around the room.

Yet it seemed that over-sensitivity wasn't his only complaint. As we talked more, he told me that he suffered from a peculiar kind of terror. What frightened him was fear itself. He was afraid of what the future might bring, dreading that some trivial incident might set off his nervous condition, driving him insane or even killing him.

He was also convinced that the family house, which he had not left for many years, had a strange and unhealthy influence on his moods and thoughts. He believed that, over the years, the very walls and turrets of the place, along with the damp mists rising from the lake below, had affected his state of mind.

He then confessed that there was also a more down-to-earth reason for the gloom that hung over him. A dearly-loved sister – his last surviving relative, who for many years had been his only companion – was seriously ill and now seemed close to death. He told me, in a bitter voice that I can still remember well, that her death would make him the last of the Usher family.

While he was telling me all of this, Lady Madeline (for that was her name) appeared suddenly at the far end of the room. She moved across it in silence, without even seeming to notice me. I gazed at her with a mixture of curiosity and dread, without really knowing why I felt that way. As the door closed behind her, I glanced over at her brother. He had buried his face in his hands, but I could see that behind his pale, unnaturally thin fingers he was crying.

Later, Usher told me that Lady Madeline's disease had baffled her doctors for a long time. She seemed to have lost all interest in life and was gradually wasting away. From time to time she would pass into a sort of trance and her body would, for a while, go as stiff and cold as a corpse. Yet, up until the day of my arrival, she had managed to hold out against staying in bed. That very evening, however, she had finally decided to take to her room. Her brother told me, with a great deal of unhappiness, that that fleeting glimpse was probably the last I would see of her – at least while she was still alive.

For several days after this, neither Usher nor I spoke of Madeline. Instead, I did my best to try to cheer him up, although I soon realized that this would be no easy task. I shall never forget the many solemn hours the two of us shared during that time. We occupied ourselves with art, music and books. Usher painted all kinds of abstract pictures, full of vague shapes that made me shudder without knowing why. He recited long, rambling poems of his own, sometimes accompanying them with haunting melodies which he played on the guitar.

We also read many strange, ancient books that, over the years, had influenced Usher's mind. Some of these described weird imaginary journeys – others contained wild philosophical ideas. The one he seemed to like best was a rare Latin work which told of some long-forgotten church's strange rituals for burying the dead.

We spent our days in this way until one evening Usher abruptly informed me that Lady Madeline had passed away. He added that he intended to keep her body for a fortnight in one of the many vaults beneath the house, before finally laying it to rest in the family burial ground. His reason for this strange decision was that the cemetery lay a long way from the house, and that newly-dead bodies in those parts were sometimes stolen to be used for medical purposes. He reminded me that his sister's unusual illness had been of special interest to her doctors, and remembering the rather sinister appearance of the doctor I had met on the stairs when I first arrived at the house, I saw nothing wrong in this seemingly harmless precaution.

At Usher's request, I helped him prepare for the burial. We placed the body in a coffin and carried it to a vault that lay deep under the part of the building where my own bedroom was. Long ago, the vault had probably been used as a dungeon. I guessed that, more recently, gunpowder must have been stored there, for the floor and walls of the passage that led to it had been coated with copper, to cover up the cracks and keep out the damp, and there were still a few traces of powder to be seen. The iron door was also covered with a layer of copper. It was extremely heavy and creaked loudly as we pushed it open.

The vault had been closed up for so long that the stale, stuffy air half-smothered the flames of our torches as we entered. Although we could see very little, we could make out that we were in a small space with no window or other opening to let in even a glimmer of light.

Having set the coffin down in this dreadful place, we lifted the lid to take one last look at Lady Madeline. I was startled to see just how much she looked like her brother. Guessing my thoughts, Usher murmured softly that they were twins and that there had always been a deep bond between them.

We didn't spend long looking at the dead woman, for there was something about her appearance that made us feel even more ill at ease than might have been expected in such a place. A touch of pink still lingered on her cheeks, and the slightest suspicion of a smile seemed to hover on her lips. Replacing the lid, we screwed it down and went out, closing the iron door firmly behind us. Then we made our way back upstairs.

My friend spent the next few days bitterly mourning the loss of his sister. During this time, a change came over him. He gave up his usual habits, and instead passed the hours roaming from room to room, walking with hurried steps. His complexion seemed paler and more deathlike than ever, but the brightness in his eyes had gone. And when he spoke, his voice quavered, as if in terror.

Now and then I sensed that some terrible secret was weighing on his mind, and that he was trying to find the courage to tell it to me. At other times, I could only think he had gone insane, for he would gaze at nothing for hours on end, deep in concentration as if listening for some imaginary sound. His mood terrified me, for I felt it starting to affect me too, making me nervous and ready to jump at the slightest noise.

I was particularly aware of these feelings one night about a week after we had placed Lady Madeline in her dungeon tomb. I had gone to bed but I could not sleep. As the hours ticked by, my nervousness increased. I did my best to persuade myself that this was simply due to the gloomy furnishings of the room. The dark tapestries on the walls and heavy curtains around the bed were swaying and rustling uneasily, stirred by the breath of a rising storm.

But it was no use. Gradually I started to tremble, and I found myself overcome by waves of terror. Struggling hard to shake off this feeling, I sat up in bed and peered into the darkness that surrounded me. I listened carefully. During breaks in the storm's noise, I thought I could occasionally make out some low and indistinct sounds, but I could not tell exactly where they were coming from. Gripped by fear, I leaped out of bed and threw on my clothes, sure that I would not get back to sleep that night. I started pacing up and down rapidly to calm my nerves.

I hadn't been on my feet for more than a few moments when I was stopped in my tracks by the sound of steps on the staircase outside. Then there was a knocking at the door. I opened it to find Usher standing outside with a lamp. He looked as pale as ever, but now there was a wildness in his eyes that really frightened me.

At that moment, though, anything was better than being alone, so I welcomed him in with relief. He entered and gazed around the room for some minutes in silence. Then suddenly he spoke. "So you haven't seen it?" he asked. "You haven't seen it, then? But you will." And with this strange utterance he hurried to one of the windows and threw it open.

The furious gust of air that blew in nearly knocked us off our feet. It was a wild night indeed, yet there was a fierce beauty to it. The wind was constantly changing direction, almost as if a whirlwind was blowing around the house. The clouds were so low in the sky that they seemed to be pressing on the building's very turrets, and they clashed against one another with terrible speed. There was no moon nor stars in sight, and no flashes of lightning. And yet the clouds and the ground beneath them were lit up by an unnatural glow that hung over the house like a shroud.

"Don't look!" I shouted at Usher, pulling him back from the window to a nearby chair. Trying to calm him, I struggled to find some rational explanation for the light we'd both seen.

"It's probably some sort of electrical effect," I said, hoping to convince myself as well as him. "Or maybe it's caused by marsh gases coming up from the lake."

He stared at me blankly. Closing the window, I picked up a book. I told him I would read to him so we could pass the terrible night together. The work I had chosen was called *The Mad Tryst*. It described the adventures of a knight in times long past. As the window sashes rattled and the storm raged outside, I began to read aloud. The story was dull and badly written, yet the moment I started reading I could see Usher hanging on my every word.

I came to a passage in which the hero of the story tries to force his way into a hermit's dwelling.

"Feeling the rain on his shoulders and fearing a storm was about to break," I read, "the knight lifted his club and smashed a hole in the wooden door. Then, thrusting his hand inside, he ripped and tore the dry wood apart, making a hollow noise that echoed through the forest."

As I finished this sentence, I paused. For a moment it seemed to me that I too could hear, from somewhere in the depths of the house, the stifled echo of the very same cracking and ripping sound the writer had described. Quickly deciding that it must have been my imagination playing tricks on me, I went on with the story.

"Once he was inside the hut," I read, "the knight could see no sign of the hermit. Instead he found himself face to face with a fierce and fiery dragon guarding a treasure of gold on a floor of silver. At once he raised his club and struck the beast down. As it fell, it let out a shriek so harsh and piercing that the knight had to cover his ears with his hands."

Here again I stopped, for, to my amazement, I was sure I could hear in the distance a long, harsh screeching noise – exactly as I imagined a dragon's shriek would sound. A shiver ran down my spine and the terror I had been trying to suppress started creeping up again. But I managed to keep my worries to myself, not wanting to make my friend any more nervous than he already was.

I wasn't sure if he had heard the sounds, but I could sense his manner had changed in the past few minutes. I couldn't see his expression, for he had gradually moved his chair around until it was facing the door of the room. But I did notice that his lips were moving, as if he were murmuring to himself. His head was hanging down on his chest, but I knew he wasn't asleep because I could see that one eye was still wide open. I noticed too that his body was gently but steadily rocking from side to side.

Taking note of all this, I returned to the story.

"And once the knight had dragged the dragon's body out of the way," I read on, "he stepped forward to lift down a huge bronze shield that was hanging on the wall. But as he did so, it fell at his feet on the silver floor with a terrible and mighty clanging."

No sooner had these words passed my lips than I heard the muffled sound of clattering metal, just as if a bronze shield had indeed fallen onto a floor of silver. Completely unnerved, I leaped to my feet. Usher, undisturbed, went on rocking. I rushed to his chair. His eyes were staring straight ahead of him, and his whole face seemed frozen. But as I reached out my hand to touch his shoulder, he shuddered all over and a sickly smile appeared on his lips. He was speaking in a low, hurried murmur, as though unaware of my presence. Bending over him, I at last managed to grasp the dreadful meaning of his words.

"Not hear it?" he was saying. "Oh yes, I hear it. I've heard it for many minutes, many hours, many days. Yet I didn't dare – miserable wretch that I am – I didn't dare – I didn't dare speak out! We have put her in the tomb alive. Didn't I tell you that my senses were unusually sharp? Oh yes – I heard her first feeble movements in the coffin. I heard them many, many days ago – and yet I didn't dare – I didn't dare say anything. And now – tonight – the story – ha! – the breaking of the hermit's door, the death-cry of the dragon, the clanging of the shield! Or should I say the opening of her coffin, the grating of the iron door, and her struggles against the coppered walls of the vault! Where can I run to? She'll soon be here. She's coming to reproach me for burying her too soon. There – isn't that her footstep I hear on the stairs? Isn't that the heavy, horrible beating of her heart?" Here, he sprang furiously to his feet and shrieked out the words as though he was pouring out his very soul.

"Listen – I tell you, she is standing outside this room right now!"

At that very moment, as if the superhuman energy with which he spoke had broken a spell, the huge ebony door suddenly swung open. And there outside, the tall figure of Lady Madeline was standing in her shroud. There was blood on her white robes, and signs of a bitter struggle showed in every part of her pitifully thin body.

For a moment she remained there, trembling and swaying in the doorway. Then, with a low moan, she fell forward into the room, lurching violently against her brother and carrying him down with her to the floor as she collapsed in death. When I leaned closer to them, I found that he was  dead too, probably carried away by the terror that he had feared for so long.

From that room, and from the house, I fled in horror. The storm was still raging wildly as I crossed the lake. Suddenly, a gleam of light shot across my path. I turned in surprise to see where it could have come from, as I knew there was nothing behind me but the big, dark house. Then I saw that the light was coming from a blood-red moon. It was shining through the crack, once almost invisible, that zigzagged down the side of the building.

And as I stood there gazing, the crack grew wider, the storm roared more wildly, the whole circle of the moon came into view, my head reeled as I saw the mighty walls of the house splitting open... Then there was a long, thunderous shouting sound, like the voice of a thousand waters. And all that remained of the House of Usher sank silently into the deep, dank lake at my feet.

# THE GOLD BUG

## PART ONE: *TREASURE HUNT*

Many years ago, I became friendly with a man called William Legrand. He came from a well-known family and had once been rich. But he had lost all his money through a series of misfortunes, and had left the family home to settle on a small island just off the eastern coast of the USA.

This island is called Sullivan's Island. It is about three miles long, but nowhere more than a quarter of a mile wide, and is mostly covered with sand. A narrow stretch of marshy water separates it from the mainland. There are no trees there, only shrubs called sweet myrtles that grow over three times the height of a man. Near the western tip is a fort occupied by soldiers. Otherwise the only buildings are a few run-down shacks used by summer visitors.

Legrand lived in a small hut he had built for himself among the myrtles near the island's eastern end. He was a well-educated, intelligent man, but he was also moody and didn't much care for other people's company. He had many books in the hut, but he didn't spend much time reading. His chief pleasures were fishing and shooting, or wandering around the island looking for shells or rare insects to add to his

fine collection. His only regular companion was
Jupiter, an old man who had once been a slave of the
family. Jupiter had been given his freedom long ago,
but nothing could persuade him to leave the man he
still called 'Master Will'.

One October evening when the weather was
unusually chilly, I decided to pay Legrand a visit. I
sailed over from the mainland, then scrambled
through the myrtles, arriving at the hut just before
sunset. No one answered when I knocked, so, finding
the key in its usual hiding place, I unlocked the door
and went in. I was pleased to see that the fire in the
grate was still giving off some heat. I took off my
overcoat and sat down in an armchair near the glowing
embers to wait for Legrand and Jupiter to come back.

They arrived soon after dark and greeted me
warmly. Jupiter bustled around, putting more logs on
the fire and getting supper ready. Legrand was in one
of his enthusiastic moods. This was partly because he
had found a rare shell on the beach, but there was
another reason too. With Jupiter's help, he had caught
a scarab beetle which he believed to be of a totally
unknown species. He said he would show it to me the
next day, so I could tell him what I thought of it.

"Why not tonight?" I asked, rubbing my hands
together in front of the blaze.

"If I'd only known you were coming!" Legrand
retorted. "But it's so long since we last saw you. How
could I have guessed you'd be here tonight? The fact is
that, as I was coming home, I met a lieutenant from

the fort. He's an acquaintance of mine so I couldn't resist showing him the bug. He was so impressed, he asked if he could take it back with him to let the other soldiers have a look. So I haven't got it to show you. But if you stay the night, I'll send Jup down for it in the morning. It's the loveliest thing you ever saw – about the size of a walnut, and brilliant gold, with two jet-black spots at one end of its back and one longer one at the other..."

"... and heavier than any bug I ever came across," Jupiter interrupted. "Ask me, and I'd say that bug is solid gold – every bit of it, inside and all."

I expected Legrand to scoff at this, but instead he merely told Jupiter not to forget about supper. Then he turned to me again. "You really might almost believe it was gold," he said. "I've never seen a brighter glow. But you'll see for yourself tomorrow. In the meantime, I can at least give you an idea of what it looks like."

So saying, he sat down to sketch his new discovery. There was a pen on the table, but nothing for him to draw on.

"Never mind," he said. "This will do." And he took a scrap of what looked like very dirty paper from his pocket, and started to draw on it. When he had finished, he handed the sketch to me.

As I took it, we heard a growling and scratching at the door. Jupiter opened it, and Wolf, Legrand's big Newfoundland dog, came rushing in. Recognizing me from previous visits, he leaped up affectionately and started trying to lick me. When he had calmed down a little, I turned my attention to the sketch. What I saw puzzled me deeply.

"I've never seen a beetle like this before," I said, after studying it for some time. "It looks more like a skull than anything else."

"A skull, do you say?" Legrand sounded surprised.

"Well, perhaps it does on paper. The two upper spots do look a little like eyes, I suppose, and the lower one could be a mouth."

I wasn't convinced. "If that's a beetle and not a skull," I told him, "all I can say is that you're not much of an artist."

I could see Legrand was annoyed by my remark, so I handed back the paper without saying anything more. He took it silently, and was about to crumple it up and throw it in the fire when something caught his eye and seemed to rivet his attention.

His face first turned red, then grew pale. He sat staring at the drawing for some minutes. Then he got up, took a candle from the table, and walked over to a chest in the far corner of the room. He sat down on the chest and started to examine the paper again, turning it in all directions but saying nothing. His actions surprised me, but I thought it better not to risk irritating him again by making any remark.

Eventually, he took a wallet from his coat pocket, put the paper carefully inside it, and locked it away in his writing desk. After that he calmed down a little, but his mind seemed to be elsewhere.

As the evening wore on, he grew more and more preoccupied. I had planned to spend the night at the hut, as I had often done before, but seeing my host's mood, I thought it better to leave. He didn't press me to stay – in fact, he shook my hand in a way that made me suspect that he was eager for me to go.

A month passed, during which I heard nothing from Legrand. Then one day, Jupiter came to visit me at my home. I had never seen him look so upset, and I immediately realized that something bad had happened.

"What's wrong, Jup?" I asked.

"It's Master Will," he said. "He's sick, very sick. He needs help. I don't know what to do."

"Sick?" I repeated. "Has he caught some disease?"

"No, no disease," replied Jupiter. "It's nothing like that. It's his mind that's wrong. I don't know what's come over him."

"Has he been acting strangely?"

"Strangely?" Jupiter echoed. "Worse than that. You'd hardly recognize him. It's almost as if he's possessed."

"In what way?" I was getting alarmed now. Jupiter made it sound as if Legrand was losing his mind. "What sort of things has he been doing?"

"Crazy things," said Jupiter in a very gloomy voice. "He's just not the same man he was. All day long he sits there scribbling odd letters and numbers that don't make any sense. And that's not all. One day he got up before sunrise and sneaked out of the house on his own. He never even told me that he was going. It was dark by the time he got back."

"Have you any idea what's on his mind?" I asked.

"Gold," said Jupiter. "All the time he thinks about gold – nothing but gold. He even talks about gold in his sleep."

"But why? What could have brought this on?"

"It's the gold bug," Jupiter replied without a moment's hesitation. "I reckon it must have bitten him. And I think I know when. It was when we first found it, by the shore. Master Will picked it up, then dropped it again like a hot coal. I could see it had hurt him, but he shouted at me not to let it get away. So I picked up a scrap of paper that was lying on the ground nearby to catch it with. I didn't want to get bitten too."

"I'm sorry to hear all this – very sorry indeed," I said, racking my brains to think of something useful to suggest. Finding nothing, I added, "But I'm not sure there's very much I can do to help."

As I spoke, the old man reached inside his coat and pulled out a crumpled envelope.

"Here, take it," he told me with a deep sigh. "It's for you."

I took the envelope and opened it. Inside, I found the following letter from Legrand. There was something about the tone of the note that made me uneasy. It didn't seem like

*Sunday, 15th November*
*Sullivan's Island*

*My dear Jonathan,*

*I'm afraid I owe you an apology for the way I behaved the last time we met. I was rude, and I'm sorry about it. The only excuse I can give is that I have not been in good health for some time.*

*Now something else has happened to disturb my peace of mind. Since I last saw you, I have had great cause for anxiety. I have something to tell you, yet I hardly know how to say it, or even whether I should mention it at all.*

*If you possibly can, come over with Jupiter at once. Do come. I need to see you tonight on urgent business.*

*Yours,*
*William Legrand*

Legrand's usual style. And I couldn't imagine what possible 'urgent business' he could have with me. Jupiter's description of his state of mind wasn't very encouraging either. I was starting to fear that his money worries had finally driven him over the edge.

I hurriedly got ready to go with Jupiter. When we reached the jetty, I noticed a scythe and three shovels, all brand new, lying in the bottom of the boat that was to take us to Sullivan's Island.

"What are you bringing those for, Jupiter?" I asked, pointing at them.

"I don't know," he said with a shrug. "Master Will told me to buy them."

A strong breeze carried us quickly over the water. We then walked the two miles to the hut. It was about three in the afternoon when we arrived, and Legrand had obviously been waiting for us eagerly. He grasped my hand with a nervous urgency that alarmed me and strengthened my suspicions about his state of mind. His face was pale, and his deep-set eyes looked strangely bright.

After some polite questions about his health, I asked him, to make conversation, whether he had managed to get the beetle back from the lieutenant.

"Oh yes," he replied, "I got it back the very next morning. Unfortunately it was dead, though – I suppose it couldn't be expected to survive long in captivity. Still, nothing will persuade me to part with that bug again. Jupiter's right about it, you know."

"In what way?" I asked, more convinced than ever that my friend was losing his mind.

"In thinking it's real gold," he said. And I was startled at how serious he sounded.

"It will make my fortune," he went on, smiling triumphantly. "I'll be able to buy back all the family possessions. That's why it means so much to me. All I have to do is put it to its proper use, and the gold will be mine."

While I tried to guess what on earth he was talking about, Legrand went to fetch the beetle from the small glass case he had put it in. It was indeed a beautiful creature, and, as Legrand suspected, probably of great value from a scientific point of view. It was covered in hard, glossy scales which really did look like burnished gold. And it was also remarkably heavy.

"I sent for you because I need your help," Legrand told me when I had finished examining the beetle. "Jupiter and I are going on an expedition to the mainland, and we need the assistance of someone we can trust."

"Does this have anything to do with the beetle?" I asked suspiciously.

"Yes," he replied bluntly, without offering any explanation. Then he added, "We must set off at once. We're heading for the hills. It'll take a couple of hours to get there from the mainland coast."

"In that case it'll be almost dark by the time we get there," I pointed out. The whole idea sounded crazy to me.

"That's no problem," he said. "We might be out all night. But we'll be back before sunrise – I promise you that."

"Wouldn't it make more sense to wait till the morning so we can get a good night's sleep first?" I suggested.

"No, we must go now," he said firmly. "Besides, I'm far too excited to sleep."

"Well, I for one don't feel like spending the night out on a wild goose chase," I told him angrily.

He seemed unperturbed. "Very well," he said. "In that case Jup and I will go alone."

I could see that his mind was made up, and there was little chance of getting him to change it. So I agreed to go with him, but only after making him promise that, once the whole ridiculous business was over, he'd come home and take at least a week's rest. Then, with a heavy heart, I got ready to leave.

We set off at about four o'clock – Legrand, Jupiter, Wolf and I. Jupiter insisted on carrying the scythe and shovels, and I couldn't help thinking it was mainly because he was afraid to let his master get his hands on them. I carried a couple of lanterns, while all Legrand had was the dead beetle, tied to the end of a long piece of string. On the way, I tried to get Legrand to say something more about the reason for the expedition, but he seemed unwilling to talk. All he would say was, "Wait and see."

We sailed over to the mainland, then set off walking in a northwesterly direction through quiet countryside. There was no sign of other people. Legrand led the way, pausing now and then to check our position in relation to certain landmarks that he must have noted on a previous visit.

We went on in this way for about two hours. Just as the sun was setting, we came to a particularly desolate area. It was a flat stretch of land near the top of a steep, wooded hill. Here and there, huge rocks loomed among the trees and deep ravines led off in various directions.

The plateau we had climbed onto was so overgrown with brambles that we would never have been able to force a way through without the scythe. Following Legrand's directions, Jupiter cleared a path to the foot of an enormous tree – one of the tallest I had ever seen.

When we reached the base of the tree, Legrand turned to Jupiter and asked him, "Do you think you could climb it, Jup?"

At first, the old man seemed taken aback by the question and for a while he didn't say anything. Instead, he went up to the huge trunk and walked slowly around it, examining it very carefully. Then at last he said, "Yes, sir. Jup can climb anything."

"Up you go, then," Legrand said. "And take this with you." He handed him the beetle.

This idea seemed to alarm Jupiter. "No," he wailed, shaking his head in fear. "Not the bug!"

"Don't be a fool," snapped Legrand. "A man your age afraid of a dead beetle!" And he thrust it at him.

Jupiter gingerly took hold of the string to which the bug was attached, taking care to keep the insect itself as far away from his body as he possibly could. Then he started to climb. Gripping the trunk tightly with his arms and legs, he pulled himself up. At first, he had only the rough bark to hold onto, and a couple of times he came close to falling. But at last he managed to struggle up to a fork 60 or 70 feet above the ground. From that point on, his task became easier, because there were several big branches to cling onto.

He climbed higher and higher until he was completely hidden from view by the dense foliage. Legrand shouted to him to keep going, and to count the branches as he went. When Jupiter called down to us that he had reached the sixth branch, Legrand told him to go one higher.

A short while later we heard Jupiter's voice. "I'm at the seventh branch," he said.

"Work your way along it as far as you can," Legrand called, his voice tense with excitement. "And tell me if you see anything that looks strange."

This peculiar request brought back my worries about my friend's state of mind, and made me all the more anxious to get him home as soon as possible. While I was thinking about how best to manage this, Jupiter's voice came again.

"I can't go on," he yelled down. "The branch is rotten."

This news seemed to plunge Legrand into despair. I'd never seen him look so dejected. I took the opportunity to suggest that we should all go home, but he didn't even hear me. Instead, he roared back at Jupiter, "Test the wood with your knife. How rotten is it?"

There was a moment's silence. Then came good news. "Actually, it's not so bad," Jupiter told us. "I reckon it'll just about take my weight."

Relief spread across Legrand's face. "Crawl along it as far as you can, and I'll give you a silver dollar," he shouted.

Jupiter must have been happy with this offer, for a few seconds later a whistle of astonishment reached us through the foliage.

"Well?" cried Legrand excitedly. "What is it?"

"A skull," Jupiter shouted back. "There's a skull on the branch."

"How's it fastened on?" Legrand wanted to know.

We could hear a scuffling and a muffled cry of surprise, then Jupiter's voice saying, "It's nailed to the branch."

Legrand looked delighted at the news, as though it only confirmed what he had expected. Then he told Jupiter to do a very strange thing.

"Now listen, Jup," he said. "Listen carefully. I want you to find the left eye of the skull. When you see it, drop the beetle through it and let it fall as far as the string will reach."

We both waited.

Although Jupiter was still hidden, we soon saw the

beetle. It appeared out of the foliage on the end of the string, glistening in the last rays of the setting sun. Legrand quickly picked up the scythe and started to clear a circle three or four yards wide beneath the dangling insect. Then he told Jupiter to let go of the string and come down from the tree.

Legrand took a wooden peg from his pocket. At the exact spot where the beetle had fallen, he pushed the peg into the ground. Next, he produced a tape-measure. Fastening one end to the tree trunk, he unwound it until it reached the peg. Then he continued in a straight line, getting Jupiter to go on ahead with the scythe to clear a passage through the brambles. Fifty feet farther on, Legrand pushed another peg into the ground and marked out a second circle, this one about four feet across, with the peg in the middle. Taking one shovel himself, he handed the others to Jupiter and me, and told us to start digging.

By now, night was falling and we had lit the lanterns. We all set to work energetically, though privately I still thought the whole business was just some crazy scheme of my friend's. As we toiled away in the lamplight, I couldn't help thinking how strange we would have looked to anyone who might have stumbled upon us in that wild and desolate place.

We worked steadily for two hours, almost without speaking. The main noise was the barking of the dog, as Wolf seemed to take a great interest in what we were doing. By that time, we had dug five feet down and found nothing. Legrand seemed surprised and upset. We took a rest, and I began to hope that we might soon be able to pack up and go home. But before long, he picked up his shovel and started digging again. We had already dug up the entire circle, so now we moved beyond its edges. We also tried deepening the hole by another couple of feet. Still nothing turned up.

At last, Legrand seemed to give up hope. He climbed out of the pit with a look of bitter disappointment on his face and put his coat back on. I said nothing, but at that moment I felt really sorry for him. At a signal from his master, Jupiter began to gather up the tools. Then we turned homeward in silence.

We had taken maybe a dozen steps when Legrand suddenly swore loudly, strode up to Jupiter and seized him roughly by the collar. Jupiter's mouth fell open in astonishment. He dropped the shovels and stumbled to his knees.

"You idiot!" shouted Legrand, hissing out the words from between clenched teeth. "Tell me now – at once. Which is your left eye?"

With a look of terror on his face, Jupiter raised his hand to his right eye and held it there, as though he feared that Legrand might take a swing at him.

"I thought so! I knew it!" Legrand shouted, letting go of Jupiter. And to our amazement, he started to skip around like a spring lamb. "The game's not over yet! We must try again!" And he led the way back to the tree.

He pulled up the peg marking the spot where the beetle had fallen and moved it about three inches to the west. He then repeated the whole operation with the tape-measure, ending up at a point several yards from the place where we had been digging. Next, he marked out another circle, slightly larger than the one before, and we again set to work with the shovels. I was terribly tired by now but, despite this, I could feel a sort of excitement building up in me. Although Legrand was behaving strangely, I couldn't help being impressed by his determination.

After about an hour's digging, Wolf began barking again. He leaped into the hole and scrabbled frantically at the soil with his paws. In a few seconds, he had unearthed a human skull and a pile of bones, along with several metal buttons and some decayed fragments of what looked like clothes made of wool. Removing a few more shovelfuls of earth, we uncovered a large knife and three or four gold and silver coins.

Jupiter could hardly restrain his joy at the sight of the money, but Legrand looked deeply disappointed and urged us to keep on digging. The words were hardly out of his mouth when I stumbled and fell. I had caught my foot in a large iron ring that lay half buried in the loose earth.

As soon as Legrand saw the ring, he seemed to forget his weariness. "Come on!" he cried, his voice tense with urgency. "Dig near the ring. Quickly!"

We now set to work in earnest. By this time, I was just as excited as the others. After ten minutes, we had brought to light an oblong wooden chest. It was about three and a half feet long, two feet broad and two and a half feet deep, and was strengthened by metal bands. On each side of the chest, near the top, were three iron rings, which would allow six people to get a firm grip on it.

Pushing and pulling together, the three of us only managed to shift the chest slightly. We quickly realized that it was far too heavy to lift from the hole. Luckily, though, the lid was only fastened by two bolts. We drew them back very slowly, trembling with anticipation.

And there before us lay a gleaming treasure worth more than we could even begin to guess. In the flickering light of the lanterns, a muddled heap of gold coins and sparkling jewels glittered and glowed, dazzling our eyes with their brightness.

I can hardly describe how I felt at that precise moment. Legrand seemed exhausted by the thrill of it all, and went very quiet. And as for Jupiter, he was simply thunderstruck. He fell upon his knees in the pit and buried his arms up to the elbows in coins and jewels. He then stayed there without moving, almost as if he was bathing in the treasure.

"And it's all because of the gold bug," I heard him mutter to himself with a deep sigh.

# THE GOLD BUG

## PART TWO: *THE KEY TO THE MYSTERY*

It was growing late, and eventually I had to point out to the other two how important it was to start moving the treasure if we were to hide it before daylight. We spent some time discussing what to do, before finally deciding to make the chest lighter by taking out two thirds of its contents. We were then able, with a bit of

difficulty, to lift it out of the hole. We hid the treasure we had removed among the brambles, and left Wolf to stand guard over it. Then we made for home with the chest as fast as we could. By the time we got back to the hut, it was one o'clock in the morning.

Although we were worn out, we only rested for an hour, then had some supper. Immediately after that, we set off once more, taking with us three large, strong sacks. We reached the pit a little before four, and divided the remaining booty as equally as we could between the sacks. Then we made our way back. We arrived at Legrand's home just as the first faint streaks of dawn were appearing over the tops of the trees.

By this time, we were thoroughly exhausted, but we were still too excited to be able to get much sleep. After three or four hours spent tossing and turning in our beds, we all got up at once, almost as if we'd arranged it in advance, and started examining the treasure.

The chest had been filled to the brim with all kinds of precious objects, and we spent the whole day and much of the next night going through its contents. There were thousands of gold coins, together making a huge amount of money. Then there were the jewels: 110 diamonds (some of them enormous), 310 emeralds (all of them very beautiful), 18 huge, glowing rubies, 21 sapphires and a single, large opal.

Besides all this, there was a vast number of solid gold objects. We counted nearly 200 rings, 30 chains, 83 crucifixes (most of them large and heavy), a big bowl engraved with vine leaves and human figures, two exquisitely decorated sword handles, and many other smaller items I can no longer remember. Finally, we found 197 superb gold watches, all studded with jewels. After carefully sorting through the whole chest, we realized we were richer than we could ever have imagined.

When our excitement had died down a little, Legrand – who could see that I was itching to know the whole story – gave me a full explanation of everything that had happened.

"You remember the night I handed you my sketch of the scarab beetle," he said, "and how irritated I was when you insisted it looked like a skull? The first time you said it, I thought you must be joking. Then I became angry, because I like to think I'm quite a good artist, and when you handed back the scrap of parchment, I was about to crumple it up into a ball and throw it in the fire."

"The scrap of paper, you mean," I interrupted.

"No," he corrected me. "It looked like paper, and that's what I thought it was at first. But in fact it was a piece of very thin parchment. It was fairly dirty, you remember? Well, just as I was crumpling it up, I happened to glance at it. You can imagine my astonishment when I found that there was a skull drawn on it.

"For a moment I was too confused to know what to think. I knew that wasn't what I had drawn. So I took a candle and went over to the far end of the room to examine the parchment more closely. Turning it over, I found my sketch on the other side, just as I had left it.

"At first, I was simply startled by the coincidence of finding the two drawings, both roughly the same size, on different sides of the sheet. But then something even stranger dawned on me. I was convinced that there hadn't been another drawing there when I made the sketch. I distinctly remembered turning the scrap over to find the cleanest spot to draw on, and I could hardly have missed seeing the skull if it had been there then.

"At the time I couldn't explain the mystery, but I knew that something odd was going on. I got up and put the parchment away, determined not to worry about it any more until I was on my own.

"When you had gone and Jupiter was asleep, I sat down to investigate the whole business methodically. I started by trying to remember how the parchment had come into my possession. We had found the bug on the shore of the mainland, about a mile east of the island. It bit me when I first touched it, so Jupiter looked around for a leaf or something to pick it up with. It was then that we both saw the scrap of paper – as we then thought – lying half-buried in the sand. I remember noticing some old pieces of wood nearby that looked like the remains of a boat.

"Well, Jupiter picked up the scrap, wrapped the beetle in it and passed it over to me. On the way home we met the lieutenant. As you already know, I gave him the insect. Then I stuffed the parchment into my coat pocket. It was pure chance that I happened to put my hand on it when I was looking for something to draw on.

"Once I had worked all this out, I soon began to make connections. We'd seen the remains of an old boat lying on the seashore, and near it we had found a piece of parchment with a skull drawn on it. This immediately made me think of pirates. Everyone knows the skull was their symbol.

"I thought it was significant, too, that the scrap was parchment, not paper. Parchment is stronger than paper, and lasts longer. It was often used to record important information."

I interrupted him at this point. "But didn't you say that the skull wasn't on the parchment when you drew the beetle? It must somehow or other have been drawn on later. So how could there be any connection between it and the boat?"

"Aha! That's the key to the whole mystery!" Legrand said triumphantly. "I knew there was no skull on the parchment when I made the sketch. And I'd watched you carefully enough while you were looking at it to know that you hadn't drawn it. Then I remembered something else. It was particularly cold that night, and we'd lit a fire. You had drawn your chair up close to it. I also remembered that just as you took the parchment in your hand, Wolf jumped up at you – and this made you lower your hand so that it was closer to the fire.

"Then it dawned on me. The skull must have been drawn in invisible ink and it was the heat of the fire that had made it reappear. As soon as this idea came to me, I immediately lit a fire and held the parchment up to the heat. At first all that happened was that the faint lines of the skull became clearer. Then I noticed something else appearing. At first sight it looked like a goat."

"A goat!" The idea was so unexpected that I couldn't help laughing out loud. "You're not going to tell me that there's a connection between goats and pirates?"

"I said at first sight," Legrand continued, sounding slightly irritated. "Looking closer, I realized it was a young goat – a kid. You must have heard of Captain Kidd, the famous pirate? It struck me that the kid might be his symbol. The way it was placed at the bottom of the parchment made it look as though it was meant to be a kind of signature.

"There was one problem, though. I couldn't see any sign of writing between the skull at the top of the parchment and the kid at the bottom. Yet I was sure that there had to be some – even though none was visible."

At this point, Legrand looked at me questioningly. "Did you ever hear people talking about the vast treasure Captain Kidd and his men were said to have buried somewhere along this coast? The stories had been around for so long and were so well-known that I felt convinced that there must be some truth in them. And now I was sure that the parchment contained the instructions explaining where to find the treasure."

"So what did you do next?" I wanted to know.

"I stoked up the fire and held the parchment to the heat again. Still no writing appeared. Then it struck me that there might be dirt covering the parchment which could be stopping the ink from showing through. So I warmed up some water and carefully wiped the surface clean."

Breaking off his story at this point, Legrand got up and went over to his desk. With a flourish, he pulled out the scrap of parchment.

"Now I'll show you what I did next," he said, heading for the kitchen. I followed, and found him putting the parchment into a tin pan with the skull facing downward. Then he placed the pan in a warm oven.

A few minutes later he took it out again, and passed the parchment over to me. This is what I saw written between the skull and the kid:

```
53‡‡†305))6*;4826)4‡.)4‡);
806*;48†8!60))85;1‡(;:‡*8†
83(88)5*†;46(;88*96*?;8)*‡
(;4*‡(;485);956*;(?*7)8!8*;4
2(5*-485);)6†8)4‡‡;1(‡9;48
081;8:8‡1;48†85;4)485†528
806*81(‡9;48;(88;4(‡?34;48)
4‡;161;:188;‡?;
```

"It looks like pure gibberish to me," I told him, handing it back. "I can't make head nor tail of it."

"It wasn't as difficult to decipher as you might think," Legrand replied. "Of course, I realized at once that some sort of code was involved, and from what I knew of Captain Kidd and his men, I didn't think it would be a particularly complicated one. I've always been good at riddles of all kinds, and I was quite sure that I would be able to solve this one.

"One problem was that all the symbols are run together, which made things more difficult. If they had been separated into words, I would have been able to look for ones made up of a single letter. And that might have told me which symbols stood for the words 'A' or 'I'.

"As it was, my first step was to see which symbols appeared most often. I discovered that the number 8 featured thirty-three times. Now, the most frequently-used letter in the English language is E. So I started off by assuming that the number 8 must stand for the letter E.

"My next step was to start looking for the most common word, which is 'the'. I went through the coded message to see if I could find any repeated combination of three symbols with an 8 at the end. And I soon found that the sequence ;48 appeared no fewer than six times. That made me suspect that the semi-colon at the start of the sequence stood for T, and that the number 4 stood for H.

"Once I had decoded the word 'the', I was able to work out where certain other words began and ended – that is, immediately before and after the ;48 sequence. I found a section that read ;48;(88 near the end of the message. Substituting the letters I already knew, this became 'THE T(EE', with the bracket in the middle standing for a letter I still had to discover. It didn't take long to deduce that it must be R, to spell out 'THE TREE'.

"Reading on, I saw that the message continued ;4(‡?34;48 and I could now decode that sequence to spell out 'THR‡?3H THE'. From there it wasn't hard to guess that the missing letters were O, U and G, making the word 'THROUGH'.

"I now had seven letters decoded. I went through the message putting them into their correct places, and looked for any combination of letters that seemed familiar. Not far from the beginning, I came across the sequence 83(88 which translated into 'EGREE'. It seemed quite likely that this formed part of the word 'DEGREE', so I took a chance and guessed that the symbol that came immediately before this sequence – it was the dagger – stood for the letter D.

"By this time, I had a third of the alphabet to work with, including many of the most common letters. From that point on, it was simply a matter of more of the same. Before too long, I had the whole message decoded."

As he spoke, Legrand handed me a piece of paper. Scrawled on it were these words:

*A good glass in the Bishop's Hostel in the Devil's Seat forty one degrees and thirteen minutes north northeast main trunk seventh branch east side shoot from the left eye of the Death's Head a beeline from the tree through the shot fifty feet out*

"It doesn't make much more sense to me than it did in code," I told him.

"At first glance, I felt the same way," he replied. "I decided to start with the bishop's hostel, thinking this might be a place I could find. I asked lots of people in the area if they knew anything about it, but no one seemed to have heard of it.

"Then I remembered that a wealthy family called Bessop had owned an estate close by on the mainland for hundreds of years. I called in there, and found an old servant woman who said she knew of a place called Bessop's Castle. Only it wasn't a castle, or a hostel come to that. It was a high rock.

"She said she could guide me there, and I promised to pay her well for doing so. We found it without much difficulty, and I sent her back home. Then I set about examining the place. The 'castle' turned out to be a wilderness of cliffs and rocks, one of which was much bigger than the rest. I scrambled up to the top of it and looked around, none too certain about what I should do next.

"While I was standing there gazing about me, I noticed a narrow ledge just below where I was standing. It was only a foot or so wide and it jutted out about eighteen inches from the rock face. There was a curve in the cliff above it that made it look rather like a chair – enough, at any rate, to convince me that I'd managed to find the 'devil's seat'.

"Once I'd understood this part of the message, the next part came to me too. I knew enough about sailors' talk to realize that the 'good glass' probably meant a telescope. And I was convinced that 'forty-one degrees and thirteen minutes' and 'north northeast' must be the directions in which I should look while sitting on the devil's seat. Thrilled by what I'd discovered, I hurried home to fetch a telescope and then returned to the rock.

"I lowered myself onto the ledge, and discovered that I could only sit on it comfortably in one particular position. I used a pocket compass to find where north northeast was, then raised the telescope to an angle I calculated as forty-one degrees and thirteen minutes above the horizon.

"I moved it up and down until a gap in the foliage of a large tree caught my eye. I could see something white in the middle of the opening, but at first I couldn't make out what it was. I adjusted the focus on the telescope and looked again. Now I could see it clearly. It was a human skull.

"I now reckoned that the mystery was as good as solved. 'Main trunk seventh branch east side' had to refer to the tree I was looking at. I took 'shoot from the left eye of the death's-head' to mean dropping a bullet through the left eye socket of the skull. 'A beeline from the tree through the shot fifty feet out' must mean a straight line drawn from the trunk of the tree to the point where the bullet fell. Extended for fifty feet, it would lead to a definite point. And that had to be where the treasure was buried."

"All very clever," I told him. "But what did you do after leaving the bishop's hostel?"

"I made a note of the exact position of the tree, then went home, taking great care to remember my route. And you know the rest."

"I suppose it was Jupiter mistaking the right eye for the left that caused us to miss the spot the first time?" I suggested.

"That's right. Of course, if the treasure had been buried where the bug fell, the difference wouldn't have mattered. But the further the string went from that point, the wider the gap became. If I hadn't been so convinced there was treasure to be found, all our hard work might have been in vain."

"But why did you get Jupiter to drop the bug through the skull's eye instead of a bullet? It looked pretty odd at the time, watching you dragging a dead beetle around on the end of a piece of string."

"Ah," said Legrand apologetically. "If you must know, I was teasing you both a little. I could see that you thought I'd lost my mind, so I decided I'd play up to your expectations. Besides, I knew the bug was heavy enough to do the job just as well as a bullet."

"That only leaves one last question – whose were the skeletons that we found in the hole?"

"I don't know the answer to that any more than you, but I can think of only one likely explanation. If it was Captain Kidd himself who buried the treasure chest, he would have needed some help. When the work was done, he might have thought it best to get rid of all witnesses. A couple of blows with a shovel while his helpers were busy in the pit – who can tell? That's one secret that will probably never be uncovered."

# MORE ABOUT EDGAR ALLAN POE

# More about
# Edgar Allan Poe

The stories retold in this book are just a few of Poe's many works. He wrote over 60 tales, covering a variety of themes, but all of them contain elements of fear, suspense or mystery. Apart from those which make up this collection, some of the best known include "The Black Cat", "Loss of Breath" and "The Murders in the Rue Morgue". In addition, Poe wrote longer fiction (such as *The Narrative of Arthur Gordon Pym*) as well as poetry and literary criticism. His most famous poem, "The Raven", is every bit as creepy as the stories in this book. Poe's stories are available in collected volumes in bookshops, and many are also now available as e-texts on the internet.

Like several of Poe's stories, "The Murders in the Rue Morgue" takes place in France. It is one of a series of tales about a French detective called Dupin. Poe was one of the very first writers to create a fictional hero who appeared in several different works. This practice later became very common, Conan Doyle's Sherlock Holmes being the most famous nineteenth-century example.

Poe's writing had a huge influence on many writers and artists of the nineteenth and twentieth centuries.

Below, there are some examples of how his work has been used in other contexts.

### Film and television

Many of the stories in this book have been made into films or adapted for television. For example, ABC and Thames Television included both "The Fall of the House of Usher" and "The Telltale Heart" in a television series called Mystery and Imagination in the late 1960s.

The best-known film adaptations of Poe's work were made in the 1960s by the British director Roger Corman. These included *The Fall of the House of Usher* (1960), *The Pit and The Pendulum* (1961) and *The Masque of the Red Death* (1964). Corman also made a film of *The Raven* (1963). Many of these feature some of the most famous horror actors of their time – Vincent Price, Ray Milland and Peter Lorre. They are now regarded as classics and are available on video and DVD.

### Comics, cartoons and games

Several Poe tales have been turned into comics. Many of these were made in the 1940s, but in the early 1990s a number were reprinted in the *Classic Tales Illustrated* series. "The Raven" and "The Pit and the Pendulum" appear in this format. A Marvel Comics version of "The Pit and the Pendulum" appeared in the 1970s and can still be found in comic stores.

Several episodes of *The Simpsons* feature re-tellings

of stories by Poe. "The Telltale Head", an episode from the first series, is loosely based on "The Telltale Heart". In the "Hallowe'en Special" from the second series, Bart and Homer act out "The Raven".

"The Dark Eye", a computer game, is based on the scenario of "The Fall of the House of Usher". It features dream sequences from "The Masque of the Red Death" and "The Telltale Heart".

### Internet

There are plenty of sites devoted to Poe. Type "Edgar Allan Poe" – or the name of any of his famous works – into your search engine and follow the links.

### Music

One of the most famous uses of a work by Poe is *The Bells*, a piece by the Russian composer Rachmaninoff for choir, singers and orchestra. Composed in 1913, it uses Poe's poem of the same name.

In the mid-1970s, rock musician and producer Alan Parsons released *Tales of Mystery and Imagination*. This contained musical versions of several stories by Poe. A later version, released in 1987, features extra tracks and is still widely available on CD.

The American composer Dominick Argento has written two works based on the life and works of Poe: the opera *The Voyage of Edgar Allan Poe* (1975-76), and the orchestral piece *Le Tombeau de Poe* ("The Tomb of Poe" – 1985).

The experimental musician Diamanda Galas made an album called *Masque of the Red Death* in 1989.

Galas makes extremely unconventional, challenging and unsettling music, and her work based on Poe's stories is no exception.

*The Fall of the House of Usher*, an opera by composer Peter Hammill, with words by Chris Judge Smith, was performed and recorded in 1991. The CD features performances by a number of well-known musicians, including Andy Bell, Sarah-Jane Morris and Lene Lovich.

ANOTHER USBORNE CLASSIC

# DR JEKYLL & MR HYDE

### FROM THE STORY BY

# ROBERT LOUIS STEVENSON

Behind the locked door of Dr. Jekyll's
laboratory lies a mystery his lawyer is
determined to solve. Why does the doctor
spend so much time there? What is the
connection between the respectable
Dr. Jekyll and his visitor, the loathsome
Mr. Hyde? Why has Jekyll changed his
will to Hyde's advantage? And who
murdered Sir Danvers Carew?

This spine-chilling retelling brings Robert Louis
Stevenson's classic horror story to life, and is
guaranteed to thrill and terrify modern readers as
much as when The Strange Case of Dr. Jekyll and
Mr. Hyde was first published over a century ago.

ANOTHER USBORNE CLASSIC

# WUTHERING HEIGHTS

### FROM THE STORY BY
## EMILY BRÖNTE

... just as I was drifting off to sleep I became aware of a loud, insistent noise. Somewhere outside, a branch was knocking against the window, scratching and thumping in time to the wailing of the wind.

Eventually I could bear it no longer. I climbed out of bed, determined to break off the branch and put an end to the noise... but instead my fingers closed on a small, ice-cold hand!

High on the windswept Yorkshire moors, an old farmhouse hides dark secrets. What is the strange history of Wuthering Heights? Why has Heathcliff, its mysterious owner, cut himself off from the world, and who is the unearthly girl wandering the moors at night? The answers bring to light a passionate tale of two generations torn apart by love and revenge.

Another Usborne Classic

# Dracula

FROM THE STORY BY

## BRAM STOKER

When the other passengers on the
stagecoach found out where Jonathan was
going, they stared at him in astonishment.
Then they started whispering in
Transylvanian and Jonathan heard some
words that he knew: *pokol* and *vrolok*. The
first word meant hell, and the second . . .
Jonathan shivered. It meant vampire.

When Jonathan Harker arrives at creepy Castle
Dracula in Transylvania, he has no idea what to
expect, but all too soon his host's horrible nocturnal
habits have him fearing for his life. . . This is the story
of a battle against the forces of evil, as the eccentric
Professor Van Helsing and his brave young friends
take on the vilest vampire in the world.